DANGEROUS TERRITORY

Rellis' lip curled, grinning. "Mostly when I see a piss-ant I just step on him."

"Rellis—" It came unexpectedly, with the sound of the screen door closing.

As Rellis turned his head sharply, the grin died on his face. Flynn stood in from the doorway. He came on a few strides and stopped, his eyes on Rellis, his right hand unbuttoning his coat.

Rellis wasn't loose now. "I . . . was just asking where you were, Flynn."

"I heard you asking."

"Listen, I didn't have any part in killing your friend."

"Rellis," Flynn said quietly, "you're a liar."

"You got no cause to say that."

Flynn moved toward Rellis. "It's said." He paused, watching Rellis' eyes. "I'm going outside. I'll expect to see you within the next few minutes . . . with your gun in your hand."

THE
BOUNTY
HUNTERS

•

Elmore
Leonard

•

A DELL BOOK

Published by
Dell Publishing
a division of
Bantam Doubleday Dell Publishing Group, Inc.
666 Fifth Avenue
New York, New York 10103

ISBN: 0-440-21306-1

Printed in the United States of America

Published simultaneously in Canada

March 1993

10 9 8 7 6 5 4 3 2 1

OPM

One

●

Dave Flynn stretched his boots over the footrest and his body eased lower into the barber chair. It was hot beneath the striped cloth, but the long ride down from Fort Thomas had made him tired and he welcomed the comfort of the leather chair more than he minded the heat. In Contention it was hot wherever you went, even though it was nearly the end of October.

He turned his head, feeling the barber behind him, and frowned at the glare framed in the big window. John Willet moved to his side and he saw the barber's right ear bright red and almost transparent with the glare behind it. Beneath the green eyeshade, Willet's face sagged impassively. It was a large face, with an unmoving toothpick protruding from the corner of the slightly open mouth, the toothpick seeming unnaturally small.

John Willet put his hand under the young man's chin, raising the head firmly. "Let's see how we're doing," he said, then stepped back cocking his head and studied the hairline thoughtfully. He tapped comb against scissors then moved them in a flitting automatic gesture close to Flynn's ear.

"How's it going with you?"

"All right," Flynn answered drowsily. The heat was making him sleepy and it felt good not to move.

"You still guiding for the soldier boys?"

"On and off."

"I can think of better ways to make a living."

"Maybe I'll stay in the shade and take up barbering."

"You could do worse." Willet stepped back and studied the hairline again. "I heard you was doing some prospecting . . . down in the Madres."

"For about a year and a half."

"You're back to guiding, now?" And when Flynn nodded, Willet said, "Then I don't have to ask you if you found anything."

For a few minutes he moved the scissors deftly over the brown hair, saying nothing, until he finished trimming. Then he placed the implements on the shelf and studied a row of bottles there.

"Wet it down?"

"I suppose."

"You can use it," Willet said, shaking a green liquid into his hand. "That sun makes the flowers grow . . . but your hair isn't flowers."

"What about Apaches?" Flynn said.

"What about them?"

"They don't wear hats. They have better hair than anybody."

"Sun don't affect a man that was born in hell," Willet said, and began rubbing the tonic into Flynn's scalp.

Flynn closed his eyes again. Maybe that was it, he thought. He remembered the first Apache he had ever seen. That had been ten years ago.

D. A. Flynn, at twenty the youngest first lieutenant on frontier station, took his patrol out of Fort Lowell easterly toward the Catalinas; it was dawn of a muggy July day. Before ten they sighted the smoke. Before noon they found the burned wagon and the two dead men, and the third staked to the ground staring at the sun . . . because he could not close his eyes with the lids cut off. Nor could he speak with his tongue gone. He tried to tell them by writing in the sand, but the marks made little sense because he could not see what he was writing, and he died before he could make them plainer. But out of a mesquite clump only a dozen yards from the wagon, his men dragged an Apache who had been shot through both legs, and there was all the explanation that was needed. He could not speak English and none of the soldiers could speak Chiricahua Apache, so the sergeant dragged him back into the mesquite. There was the heavy report of a revolving pistol and the sergeant reappeared, smiling.

The hell with it, Flynn thought.

He felt the barber's fingers rubbing hard against his scalp. His eyes were still closed, but he could no longer see the man without the eyelids. He heard the barber say then, "You're starting to lose your hair up front."

Willet combed the hair, which was straighter than usual with the tonic, brushing it almost flat across the forehead, then began to trim Flynn's full cavalry-type mustache. The thinning hair and dragoon mustache made him appear older, yet there was a softness to the weather-tanned face. It was thin-lined and the bone structure was small. Dave Flynn was a month beyond his thirty-first birthday, but from fifteen feet he looked forty. That's what patrols in Apache country will do.

"Hang on," John Willet said, moving around the chair. "I see a couple of wild hairs." He took a finer comb from that shelf and turning back to Flynn he looked up to see the small, black-suited man enter the shop.

"Mr. Madora."

Flynn opened his eyes.

Standing the way he was, just inside the doorway with his thumbs hooked into vest pockets, Joe Madora could be mistaken for a dry-goods drummer. He was under average height and heavy, his black suit clinging tightly to a thick frame, and the derby placed evenly over his eyebrows might have been a size too small. His mustache and gray-streaked beard told that he was well into his fifties and probably too old to be much good with the pistol he wore high on his right hip. But Joe Madora had been underestimated before, many times, by Apaches as well as white men. Most of them were dead . . . while Joe was still chief of scouts at Fort Bowie.

He stood unmoving, staring at Dave Flynn, until finally Flynn said, "What's the matter with you?"

Madora's grizzled face was impassive. "I'm trying to figure out if you got on a fancy-braid charro rig under that barber cloth."

"It takes longer than a year and a half to go Mexican." Flynn nodded to the antlers mounted next to the door. "There's my coat right there."

Madora glanced at the faded tan coat. "You're about due for a new one."

"I'm not the dude you are."

"You bet your sweet tokus you're not."

Flynn smiled faintly, watching the man who had taught him everything he knew about the Apache. The comical-looking little man who could almost read sign in the air and better than half the time beat the Apache at his own game. He had learned well from Joe Madora, and after he had resigned his commission, it was Joe who had recommended him and saw that he got a job as a contract guide.

"I hear you're back for more," Madora said.

"You know of an easier way to make money?"

"Just two. Find gold or a rich woman."

"Well, I've given up on finding gold."

"And no woman 'ud have a slow-movin' son of a bitch like you, so you don't have a choice at that."

John Willet said, "Joe, let me trim your beard. Be done here in a minute."

Madora nodded and eased himself into the other barber chair. "Where's Irv?"

"Irv went up to Willcox to get something for his wife . . . coming in on the train."

"That's good," Madora grunted. "He's a worse barber than you are." He looked at Flynn then. "I heard about your new job. Taking that kid down into the Madres . . ." He stopped, seeing Flynn glance toward the barber. "John, you keep your ears plugged."

"I never did pay attention to what you had to say," Willet answered.

To Madora, Flynn said, "How did you find out?"

"I been guiding for Deneen. I heard him talking to this Bowers kid. Did he talk it over with you yet?"

"This morning for a minute. He kept reminding me I didn't have to take it, saying, 'You can back out,' using those words. Then he said, 'Think it over and come back later.'"

Madora smiled in his beard. "What about Bowers, did you see him?"

Flynn shook his head. He said then, "In the war we had a division commander by that name."

"Maybe he's a kin."

"What kind is he?"

"If you keep him from wettin' his pants he might do."

"How old?"

"Twenty-one . . . -two."

"West Point?"

"They all are . . . that doesn't mean anything. He's been out here a year and that's Whipple Barracks. He looks brevet-conscious. He wants to move up so bad he can taste it . . . and he's afraid going away on this job might get him lost in the woods."

"It could get him a promotion."

"It could get him killed, too. But he thinks it's more a job for a truant officer than a cavalryman. He said to Deneen, 'Sir, isn't bringing an old Indian back more a task for the reservation agent?'"

"Did you tell Bowers what it's all about?"

"He didn't ask me."

Flynn shook his head. "It doesn't make sense."

"You ought to be used to that; you've worked for Deneen

before," Madora said. "His naming Bowers doesn't make sense . . . though he must have a reason. But it's plain why he's sending you."

"Why?"

"You know as well as I do. He wants to make you quit again. You've done it twice before. Maybe he thinks one more will finish you for good."

"What do you think?" Flynn asked.

"I don't blame you for anything you did before. Deneen's Department Adjutant . . . with more weight than you got. When he says dance, you dance, or else go listen to a different tune. I wouldn't blame you too much if you backed out of this one. Only I think it can be done. I think you just might be able to drag Soldado Viejo—the old Indian, as the kid calls him—back to San Carlos."

"Two of us?"

"Two make less noise."

"Give me a better reason."

"Because I taught you what you know. And I'll give you one more," Madora added. "Because you might be mad enough to do this one just so you can throw it back in Deneen's face."

Flynn smiled. "You sound like you want to go."

"Maybe I should."

"Maybe you volunteered"—Flynn was still smiling—"but they said it wasn't something for an old man who looked like he was standing in a hole."

Madora shook his head. "I was wrong. You'll last down there about a day and a half."

"I've lasted ten years so far . . . plus three in the war when I didn't see you around."

"I was watchin' the frontier for you sword-clickin' bastards back East."

"About three thousand miles from Lee."

Madora was composed. "David," he said quietly. "All during that war of yours we had us a Mimbre named Soldado Viejo . . . the same one you're supposed to bring home.

And I'll tell you something else. Bobby Lee, in his prime, couldn't rear-guard for Soldado if all the old Mimbre raided was whorehouses."

John Willet had looked from one to the other, trying to piece the conversation into some sense. Now he put down his comb and scissors and offered a hand mirror to Flynn.

"See how it looks," he said.

His gaze went to the window, idly, and he watched a man come out of the Republic House and start diagonally across the street toward the barbershop. Over the thick green lettering that read WILLET'S from the street side, he watched the man approach; long strides, but weaving somewhat, carrying a rifle in his right hand and saddlebags over his left shoulder. Then he recognized the man.

"God, I hope he hasn't been drinking."

Neither Flynn nor Madora had noticed him yet.

Willet spoke hurriedly, watching the man reach the plank sidewalk. "That's Frank Rellis . . . sometimes he acts funny when he's had a drink, but don't pay any attention to him."

Flynn, holding the mirror, glanced up. "What?"

But Willet was looking toward the door. "Hello, Frank . . . be with you in a minute."

Frank Rellis stood in the doorway swaying slightly, then came in and unslung the saddlebags, dropping them onto the seat of a Douglas chair next to the door. He eyed the occupied barber chairs sullenly; a man about Flynn's age, he wore range clothes: a sweat-stained hat, the curled brim close over his eyes, leather pants worn to a shine and a cotton shirt that was open enough to show thick dark hair covering his chest. His pistol was strapped low on his thigh and he still held the rifle, a Winchester, pointed toward the floor.

He looked at Willet. "Where's Irv?"

"Irv had to go to Willcox," John Willet said pleasantly. "I'll be with you in a minute . . . take a chair."

"I don't have a minute."

Willet smiled. "Frank, this being herd boss keeps you on the go, don't it?"

Rellis looked at the barber impassively. His deep-set eyes were half closed from drink and an apparent lack of sleep and a two days' beard stubble made his heavy-boned face menacing. "I said I don't have a minute."

Willet smiled, but now it was forced. "I'm finishing up, then I have to trim this here gent's beard"—he nodded to Joe Madora—"and I'll be with you."

"You can do better than that."

"Frank, I don't see any other way . . ."

"I do . . . you're taking me right now."

"Frank . . ."

"You can finish them up after."

Flynn glanced from Rellis to Madora. The chief of scouts was watching Rellis closely. "Are you in a hurry?" Madora said then.

Rellis ignored him, moving toward the first chair. He stopped at the footrest, in front of Flynn's boots. The mirror was still in his hand, but Flynn was looking over it at Rellis.

"You look prettier'n a French pimp," Rellis said. "Now get out of the chair."

Flynn felt the sudden flush of anger come over his face, but he took his time. His eyes left Rellis as he raised the mirror and studied his reflection, and he was surprised that his anger did not show. Perhaps the brown face had a reddish tint to it, but that was all. Then he said, quietly, "John, you're a little uneven right in through here"—his left hand following the part—"let's try parting it a little higher."

"Looks fine to me," Willet said uneasily. "That's the way you always wear it."

"I want to try all kinds of styles," Flynn said evenly, "before I get old and set in my ways and have to live with it the rest of my life." He looked at Rellis, whose mouth had tightened. "I've got all afternoon. You can try parting it on the other side, then in the middle, then if you run out of ideas get your book out and look up a new one."

There was a silence and suddenly a brittle tension that was ready to break. Rellis' jaw tightened and colored a deeper red beneath the beard stubble. His body was stiff as if poised to make a move.

And then Joe Madora laughed. It was a soft chuckle, but it split the silence.

Rellis turned on him. "Are you laughing at me!" His face was beet-red now.

Madora's smile straightened and suddenly his dark face was cold and dead serious. He said to Rellis, "If you're not man then you shouldn't drink that lizard-pee they pass off as whisky over at the Republic."

Rellis didn't move. Flynn felt the tension and it made him ease up straighter in the chair. He looked at Rellis standing on the edge of his nerves gripping the Winchester tightly, cradled under his arm now. Rellis' eyes were wide with disbelief, staring at the little man with the beard . . . a head smaller than he was, older, and wearing his pistol in a high, awkward position. But Madora looked back at him calmly and something stopped Rellis at the peak of his anger.

"Mister," Flynn said now, and waited until Rellis looked at him. "You don't need a shave as bad as you think you do. Maybe you better get while your luck's still holding out."

Amazement was on Rellis' face, but he was near the end of his patience and the anger was plain on his face. "What's your name?" he said.

"Flynn."

"We ever met before?"

"I doubt it."

"Are you going to get out of that chair, or do I pry you out with this?" He raised the Winchester slightly.

"You raise that another inch," Flynn said calmly, "I'll kill you."

Rellis stopped. He looked at the long barber cloth that covered Flynn to the knees, smooth striped cotton that told nothing.

"You're bluffing."

"There's one way to find out."

Rellis glanced quickly at the antlers next to the door. A

tan coat hung there; a gun belt could be beneath it, but it could also be in Flynn's hand beneath the cloth.

John Willet's face turned paler under the eye shade. He said, his voice faltering, "Gentlemen, please . . ." But that was all.

Rellis moved suddenly toward the chair, but Flynn's boot kicked out in the same motion and caught him in the pit of the stomach. Rellis went back with a rip up his shirt front where Flynn's spur had slashed, and as he staggered back, Flynn came out of the chair and swung the hand mirror hard against the side of Rellis' head while his right hand wrenched at the Winchester.

The rifle barrel swung back toward Rellis, even while his hand was still on the stock, and came down across his skull. He didn't go down, but staggered backward with Flynn pushing him toward the open door, and in the doorway Flynn stopped, holding the rifle, while Rellis kept going, stumbling, until he landed in the dust on his back and rolled over. He was raising himself to his knees when his saddlebags came flying out to catch him full in the face and knock him flat again.

Flynn turned back into the shop and placed the rifle against the wall below the antlers. "Give him his rifle back when he gets some sense," he said to John Willet.

Joe Madora came out of the chair. "Some other time, John. You took a mite too nervous to be wielding scissors." He nodded to the broken glass from the hand mirror. "David, you just acquired seven years of the worst kind of luck."

Flynn paid Willet, who took the money silently, then moved to the antlers. He took down his coat, then lifted off his gun harness and passed his arm through the sling so that the holster hung well below his left armpit, the long-barreled .44 extending past his belt. He put on the tan coat, faded, bleached almost white. His light Stetson was sweat-stained around the band and he wore the stiff brim straight, close over his eyes. Putting it on, he said, "We'll see you again, John."

Willet said now, "He's not going to forget that. Dave, you don't know that man."

Madora said, "But he knows Dave now."

Two

●

They rode out of Contention toward the cavalry station which was two miles north, up on the San Pedro. It was a one-troop post and Flynn wondered why it had been chosen for the meeting place. He had been working out of Fort Thomas since his return, and Bowers was from Whipple Barracks. But that was like Deneen. He'd pick it so you would wonder. Deneen, the departmental adjutant, whom he'd known for a long time. Too long. Since Chancellorsville. And there was a day at Chancellorsville that he would never forget. Madora had said once that you ought to take a good look at Deneen because he was one of the few honest-to-God full-blooded sons of bitches left.

They rode relaxed, walking the mares, Flynn on a buckskin and Madora on a chestnut. It was close to four o'clock and already the sun was low off to the left, a long crimson streak above the colorless sierra of the Catalinas.

Madora said, "Remember Anastacio Esteban?"

Flynn looked up, surprised. "Very well."

"He came through here yesterday with about the whole tribe. Four or five wagons of big and little Estebans hanging on every place you looked."

"Here? They live down in Sonora. Soyopa."

"I know it," Madora said. "They were up the line for some shindig. You know Anastacio made a lot of friends when he was packin' mules for the army. It don't take much to get him back for a celebration."

Flynn said, "I came through Soyopa. I was digging just southeast of there and stopped off on my way back. Anastacio had me spend the night at his dobe."

"He mentioned he saw you."

"His brother Hilario is the alcalde now. Least he was six months ago when I passed through."

Madora nodded. "The quiet one."

"Unlike his brother," Flynn said. "He wasn't along, was he?"

"No; his daughter was. Did you meet her?"

"I think so."

"You don't think so about her. You either did or you didn't."

"Anita?"

"Nita," Madora said. "She could stand a few more pounds, but she's much woman the way she is."

"She was along?"

"Taking her father's place. They passed through here just yesterday. You might catch up with them . . . depending when you leave."

"We might," Flynn said.

He had become acquainted with the good-natured Anastacio while still in the army, during the time Anastacio transported supplies for them; Anastacio the mule skinner, the arriero, who talked to his animals as if they were his children, and drank mescal as if it were water. But he had not met the others until he passed through the pueblo of Soyopa. They had not come up into Arizona to work as Anastacio had done. Hilario, the quiet one. And Nita, whom one remembered well. Perhaps he would see them again.

"Deneen's here already," Madora observed, as they rode into the quadrangle of Camp Contention; a scattering of cottonwoods behind a row of drab, wind-scarred adobes, a flagpole, then a long low stable shed facing the adobes.

"That's his bay over there in the end stall the trooper's wipin' down," Madora said. "When Deneen's standin' next to it you got to blink your eyes to tell which is the genuine horse's-ass, and then you can never be dead sure."

At the end of the stable shed, a dozen or more figures sat about a smoking fire. The sun was behind them and Flynn could not make out who they were until he put his hand up to shield the sun glare.

"My boys," Madora said.

Flynn recognized them then—Coyotero Apaches, working for the army as trackers. The Apaches looked toward them then and one of them stood up and waved. He wore a faded issue shirt, but it lost its regulation worn with the rest of his attire. Red cotton headband and gray breech clout, and moccasin leggings that reached his thighs.

Madora said, "You remember him?"

"Three-cents," Flynn said. "He worked with me awhile."

"That red son's better than a bloodhound," Madora said.

A sign marked the adobe headquarters. Black lettering on a whitewashed board to the right of the door: TROOP E— SIXTH U.S. CAVALRY.

A trooper who had been at parade rest by the door took their reins and they went inside.

By the left wall, an officer, holding a kepi in his hand, came up quickly off the bench that was there and Flynn knew that this was Bowers. He glanced at the sergeant seated behind the desk and nodded, then looked back at the officer. A young man—no, he looked more a boy—above medium height, red hair cropped close and a pinkish clean-lined face with a serious set to it. His dark brown eyes held the question, though it was plain he was trying to seem incurious.

"Bowers?"

The young man nodded.

"Dave Flynn. You know Joe Madora."

The officer nodded again, taking the outstretched hand. His grip was firm and he returned Flynn's close inspection as they shook hands.

"We had a divisional commander named Bowers."

"He was my father."

"Good soldier."

"Thank you."

Then Flynn beckoned to the door leading into the post commander's office. "Is Deneen in there?"

Bowers nodded. "With Lieutenant Woodside."

"Have you seen him yet?"

"Only for a few minutes."

"He hasn't explained anything, then."

"I don't see the necessity of an explanation," Bowers stated. "I've already received my orders."

"May I see them?"

Bowers hesitated.

"Look, I'm on your side."

He drew a folded paper then from inside his jacket. "You are mentioned here," Bowers said quietly. "I assumed, though, that this would be discussed in a more private manner."

"I won't tell a soul," Flynn said. He glanced at Bowers' serious face and wanted to smile, but he did not.

Madora moved next to him then, to look over his shoulder. "That's a nice hand," he said.

Flynn held it close to his face. "I don't smell any perfume on it."

"Well, don't get it too close or you're liable to smell something else," Madora said. They read the orders in silence.

From: A. R. L. Deneen, Col.
          Dept. Adjutant, Department of Arizona
          In the field, Camp Contention, Arizona Terr.

To: Regis Duane Bowers, Second Lt.
          6th Cav. Reg.
          Whipple Barracks, Prescott, Arizona Terr.
Subject: Transfer and Reassignment   17 Oct. 1876
   As of this date, R. D. Bowers is formally assigned to the office of the Departmental Adjutant, Department of Arizona, and is hereby instructed to report to Camp Contention, Arizona Terr., for detailed instructions concerning the following outlined orders:

1. Within one week, or, before 25 Oct., R. D. Bowers will have made preparations for extended patrol.
2. R. D. Bowers will contact one D. Flynn, civilian contract guide. However, herenamed contract employee is free to decline assignment. Substitute, if needed, will be selected by the office of the Department Adjutant.
3. R. D. Bowers and civilian guide will proceed to that section of Sonora (Mexico) indicated at a future date.
4. Aforementioned are to make contact, without show of arms, with one Soldado Viejo, hostile Mimbreño Apache, and return said hostile to Apache Agency, San Carlos, Arizona Terr.
5. R. D. Bowers is warned that if detained by Mexican authorities, because of the nature of the assignment he will not be recognized by the United States as a lawful agent.
6. The subject matter contained herein is of the strictest confidential nature.

   The office of the Department Adjutant extends its heartiest wish for a successful undertaking.

                        A. R. L. DENEEN
                        Department Adjutant

   Madora said, "That last line's the one."
   Flynn returned the sheet to Bowers and moved to the bench; sitting down, hooking a boot heel on the edge, he made a cigarette and took his time lighting it, then exhaled the smoke leisurely, studying the young officer who was trying to appear composed, trying to look West Point. And it

was plain that the orders meant very little as far as he was concerned.

This was the man he would take across the Rio Grande— which they would call the Bravos then—to find Soldado, a broncho Mimbre, who had been fighting longer than Bowers or he had lived. Four dollars a day to guide a new lieutenant with only one year of frontier station behind him. To take him across sun-beaten nothingness and into scrambling rock-strewn puzzling never-ending canyons in search of something that would probably not be there. But always with eyes open, because the Apache knows his business. He knows it better than anyone else. How to kill. That simple? Yes, that simple, he thought. That's what it boils down to. That's what it is from where you're standing, so that's what you call it. Four dollars a day. More than a lieutenant makes. His uniform compensates for the low pay rate . . . though he could die naked as easy as not.

He heard Madora say, "What's he got on you?"

"I beg your pardon?" Bowers said, startled.

"He must a caught you with his old lady."

Bowers looked at him steadily, but said nothing.

Flynn took his hat off, leaning back, and felt the adobe cool against the back of his head. "Mister," he said to Bowers, "what do you think?"

"About what?"

God, the calm one. He's tensed-up being calm. "About your orders."

"You almost answer your own question. They are orders. Under the circumstances I doubt if an opinion would affect them one way or the other."

Madora grinned. "Look out, Dave. You got yourself a serious one."

"I don't believe this concerns you in the least," Bowers said coldly.

There was silence. Flynn watched the lieutenant grip his hands behind his back and walk to the single window. Flynn said to the back, "Do you know what you're talking about?"

Bowers turned on him sharply. "Mr. Flynn, I assure you I am capable of interpreting a military order. It is a precise, unadorned, quite literal description of a specific assignment which I have been trained to obey without question, without hesitation. Since my opinion is of no value, I see little reason in discussing it . . . especially with a person who is in no way related to the order in question. Is that quite clear?"

"Very clear, Mr. Bowers." Colonel Deneen stood in the doorway of the post commander's office. Lieutenant Woodside could be seen behind him. "And I might say unduly modest of you. Your opinion is worth . . . something."

He hesitated, his eyes roaming over the group in the outer office. He was a man of medium height, in his early forties, carefully dressed, from the trace of white showing above his collar to the highly polished black boots and silver spurs that chinged softly as he moved into the room. And though he took only a few steps, a faint limp was noticeable, a favoring of the right foot as he put his weight on it. One hand picked idly at the front of his tunic, as if removing invisible lint, and he looked at the three men closely, individually, as if to command their attention.

"At ease, Mr. Bowers." He nodded to Madora, who stood relaxed with thumbs in vest pockets, then his eyes went to Flynn and stopped there. Flynn had not moved his position. He leaned against the wall with a half-boot still hooked on the edge of the bench, his arm resting idly on the raised knee and the extended hand holding the stub of cigarette. He drew on it as Deneen looked toward him.

"Don't get up, Flynn."

Dave Flynn returned his stare, looking up at the smooth features, dark hair well combed and shining. He dropped the cigarette then, but did not step on it. He glanced at Woodside, the post commander. "Don, good to see you again." Then back to Deneen—"How's the foot, Colonel?"

For a moment the face tightened and the dark eyes did not blink, holding squarely on Flynn, as if waiting for him to say more, but Flynn remained silent. The face relaxed then and Deneen said, "Very well, thank you."

There was the hint of a smile playing at the tips of Flynn's mustache. "That's good. Sometimes those old wounds start aching, especially when the weather's damp."

"Fortunately the climate is uncommonly dry."

"Fortunately."

"I can't say I expected to see you here."

"I don't imagine you did."

"You know why you were asked, of course."

"As well as you do."

"Because of your knowledge of the country. I'm told you've been on a mining venture down there for something like a year and a half. I assume it was unsuccessful, or you would not have returned to scouting. Did you see signs of Soldado Viejo?"

"There are always signs."

"And less cryptically, that means what?"

"The dead."

"I suppose the Mexican government has done little."

"On my way up I talked to a man in Soyopa who said that Porfirio Diaz was sending police to help them. They were expected any day."

"Rurales?"

Flynn nodded.

"His newly formed police. Bandits to fight bandits."

"Maybe that's the way," Flynn said.

"What about the scalp bounty?"

"The government's still paying it if you're man enough to take an Apache's hair."

"I'm told there's an American outlaw down there making something of a success of scalp hunting. Lazair. Have you heard of him?"

"He was pointed out to me once."

"Where?"

"In Guazapares, over a year ago. At that time scalps had to be taken to Guazapares for the bounty. Lazair rode in with some of his men and I saw him at a distance. I saw his face before that on wanted dodgers up here."

"How does he get along with the authorities?"

Flynn shrugged. "I don't know. Everybody seems afraid of him."

"I'm told he's now trying quite eagerly for Soldado's scalp."

"He should, it's worth five hundred pesos," Flynn said. "Are you suggesting we go to him for help?"

Deneen smiled faintly. "If you were making a business of scalping Apaches, would you think kindly of someone appearing to take them away?"

"I was going to remind you of the same thing."

"I'll take the responsibility of my own reminding."

Flynn shrugged his shoulders, saying nothing.

"I will mention again," Deneen said politely, "that you are not obligated in any way to take this assignment."

"What about Bowers?"

"That is not your concern."

"I mean nothing personal, but there are other officers with considerably more experience who might have been chosen." He glanced at Bowers as he said it and saw the young officer stiffen, as if anxious to reply.

Deneen said, "Do you imply that you won't go if Lieutenant Bowers does?"

"Of course not. I just don't see why you'd send an inexperienced man on a job like this."

"And how do you gain this experience if you never take the field?"

"Tracking Soldado in his own element isn't exactly just taking the field."

"We're not going to debate it. You either go or you don't go."

"I'd like to speak to you alone."

"I haven't the time. Are you going?"

Flynn hesitated, then nodded his head.

"You will leave in the morning. The quartermaster sergeant will issue your ammunition if you use a Springfield; otherwise you supply your own."

"I'm aware of all that."

"Then there's no reason to detain you," Deneen said, and turned abruptly to Bowers. "Lieutenant, step into the office."

The sun had dropped below the horizon line of the Catalinas and they rode back to Contention in the silent dusk, Flynn thinking, reminding himself that he was in it now, and that was that.

"He was almost half decent for a minute," Madora said. "Then the ninety-nine per cent bastard started to show."

"You've got to hand him that," Flynn said. "He's consistent." Flynn was silent, riding, following the sway of his mount. Then, "Joe, where does he get his authority for this?"

"I hadn't thought of it."

The orders said the army wouldn't recognize us. If there was an agreement with Mexico, there'd be an expedition."

"With a lot of noise," Madora added. "And you'd never find Soldado."

"That's not the point. What does the general say about this? I don't think it's something that can be kept from him."

"Deneen's a talker," Madora said. "Maybe he can explain it so it sounds legal."

"Maybe." Flynn shrugged it off then, saying, "What are you going to do now?"

"I'm leadin' Deneen's grand tour of post inspections. With Three-cents and his Coyoteros along to add color."

"You could do worse."

"Like what?"

It was dark when they turned off Commercial Street onto Stockman, riding past the Republic House on the corner. They were both staying there and they boarded their horses at the livery stable behind the hotel, on Stockman. They dismounted in front of the wide doorway framing the darkness inside.

"I wonder where the man is?" Madora said. He stopped just inside, blinking his eyes.

Behind him, Flynn said, "Seems to me there was a lantern on a nail along the boards there."

"Over here?" Madora moved into the darkness.

"This side of the first stall."

Madora's hand went into his coat pocket and came out with a match. He scratched it against the board partition and just ahead of him Flynn saw a yellow flare and Madora's face close to the boards.

And the heavy, ringing, solid slam of the rifle report was there with the match flare. Flynn went down instinctively. The match went out and he heard Madora gasp as if he'd been hit hard in the stomach, and the sound of his weight falling against the partition.

"Joe!"

Flynn was rising. Three shots then in quick succession in the close stillness and he went down flat, hearing the horses scream, knowing they had been hit. In front of him, Madora's mare fell heavily and did not move, but his own broke away and veered out into Stockman Street. His pistol was in his hand, but there was nothing, only the darkness and the stabled mounts moving nervously, bumping the boards and nickering.

Suddenly the rear door, not more than fifty feet away, swung open with the sound of hoofs striking boards and packed earth and momentarily horse and rider were framed against the dusk, pushing through as the door swung open only part way. Flynn fired, the heavy revolver lifting in his hand, and then horse and rider were gone and he could hear the hoofbeats outside, on the street beyond the livery.

Madora was breathing with his mouth open, his chest rising and falling with a wheezing sound. Flynn's hand went over him gently until he felt the wet smear of blood just above his waist at his side.

"Joe, you'll be all right. It probably went clean through you."

Madora tried to answer, but he could not. He was breathing harder, gasping.

There were footsteps behind them.

"What happened?"

Then more steps on the packed ground and a familiar voice. It belonged to the barber, John Willet.

"Soon as I seen him I knew . . . tearing up Commercial like that. I didn't even hear the shots and I knew."

Someone said, "Who?"

"Who do you think!" Willet's voice was edged with nervousness. "Frank Rellis. My God, he's done it now. . . ."

Three

●

Late in the afternoon the sky changed to pale gray and there was rain in the air, the atmosphere close and stifling, and a silence clung heavily to the flat colorless plain. The distant peaks to the east, the Dragoons, rose gigantically into the grayness, seeming nearer than they were, and the towering irregular crests were lost in the hazy flat color of the sky.

The sudden threat of rain was relief after the relentless sun glare of the morning. They had traveled through it saying little, their eyes heavy-lidded against the glare. Flynn's searching, from habit swinging a slow wide arc that took in every brush clump and rise, then lifting to the rimrock and squinting for the thin wisp of smoke that would be almost transparent in the sunlight, or the mirror flashes that no white man could read, and half expecting one or the other to be there—because you never knew. There were reservations; still, you never knew.

Flynn followed the sway of his horse loosely, a dun mare that he had bought last night, listening to the squeak of saddle leather. His hat was straight across his eyebrows and he seemed tired, listless; yet his eyes never ceased the slow swing over the valley. Often he would slip his boots from the stirrups and let his legs hang free. All things become routine. Relax, and be watchful at the same time. Relax only, and in Apache country it will kill you.

He thought about Joe Madora and he could still hear the wheezing sound of his breathing. The crowd that had formed almost out of the air. First they were alone, then there were voices, dozens of voices, and one that he recognized. John Willet's voice. He had heard John Willet very clearly say the name Frank Rellis. He had told Bowers about it before they started out that morning. Bowers said he was sorry, that was about all.

Bowers wore civilian clothes now, a gray broadcloth suit that he had worn on furlough perhaps a year or two before and now was too small for him.

The doctor had worked on Madora a long time, half the night, and stayed there the rest of it, up in the hotel room where they'd carried the wounded man. He'd stop the bleeding, then it would start again and he'd work at the wound, applying compresses. Madora was unconscious by then, his eyes closed lightly as if ready to snap open at any moment. Flynn had watched the face more than he did the doctor's hands working at the middle of Madora's body, because he expected the face to become colorless and the eyes to open. He was sure they would open, because almost every dead man he could remember had been lying with his eyes open. He had placed small stones over the eyelids when he had the time. That was a strange thing. No, that's why you remember them. There were others with eyes closed that you don't remember.

But Madora's face remained calm, and though the bearded skin was pale, it did not become drained of all of its color.

Flynn slept for an hour before dawn and when he awoke and pulled on his boots and strapped on his gun, the doctor told him that the old man had a chance to live, but he wouldn't advise making any hotel reservation in his name.

They camped early because of the rain threat and rigged

their ponchos into a lean-to. But the rain never came. And later on, when the moon appeared, its outline was hazy and there were few stars in the deep blackness.

Flynn lay back with his head on his saddle and lighted a thin Mexican cigar. In three and a half days we'll be there. Soyopa. And then we will watch and get to know this Apache and see if there is a pattern to the way he lives. What are his limitations? Where is his weak spot?

He stopped suddenly and blew the smoke out slowly and smiled to himself. What's the hurry? As old as he is, he'll probably be there years after you're gone. Luck doesn't last forever, you know. It stretches so far and when you're not looking there's a *pop* and it's all over and you don't know what hit you. He smiled again. But that's if you're lucky. That's how luck runs out if you're lucky.

He relighted the cigar and it was a soft glow in the corner of his mouth. Lying on his back, looking up into the darkness, his hand moved the cigar idly from one side of his mouth to the other, half biting and half just feeling the strong tobacco between his lips. He could see the girl's face clearly. Nita Esteban. He had thought of her because he had thought of Soyopa. The lines of her face were sensitive, delicate, and her lips parted slightly as she smiled. She had worn a red scarf over her slim shoulders and held the ends of it in front of her. He remembered the red scarf well. What would she be, seventeen? Not much older.

He watched the eternity of the sky. The dark was restful, but the vastness was cold and made you draw something close to you. His head rolled on the saddle and he saw Bowers' form across the small fire. He's trying to figure out what the hell he's doing here, Flynn thought.

Maybe we'll catch the Estebans. That would be good. Then we could talk about all those things Deneen brought up and be familiar with them before reaching Soyopa.

Bowers is honest, though. He doesn't like something and he shows it. He doesn't like this, but he doesn't realize what is involved. He thinks it is dull routine that will keep him out of the promotion light for too long. Probably he has been talking to Deneen and Deneen had told him to keep an eye on me because, well, even though Flynn was an officer at one time, he's not the most reliable man in the world, you see he resigned his commission because he was hotheaded and maybe a little afraid of what was to come. Those things happen.

Bowers thinks all the time and he doesn't smile.

And his dad was Division Commander over Deneen during the war. What's that got to do with Bowers being here now? Something. You can bet your best plugged peso, something.

You smiled most of the time at first, he told himself. You smiled to show you were eager. A smile shows sincerity. Warmhearted, clean-souled, open-minded . . . and inexperienced.

Flynn thought of the gray morning in April when he had crossed the Rappahannock with Averell's Brigade. Seventeen years old and a second lieutenant because his father knew somebody. He remembered Deneen, who had been his captain then, his first captain, saying, nodding to the hills, "They're up there. Those gray-coated, sorghum-eating manure spreaders are up there. We get them before they get us." He had been close to Deneen and he had smiled, because Deneen was a captain and had taken them through training and he talked like a cavalryman was supposed to talk.

They met Fitz Lee, who was part of Stuart's sabers, and almost cut him to pieces, but they couldn't finish it because the rebel pickets were too close and by then the alarm had been spread. It was a good day and he had thought: This won't be so bad.

Then Chancellorsville. The third night it had been raining hard, but it stopped a matter of minutes after their patrol came in. The rebel artillery started up shortly after this. Whitworths pouring it down from the thicketed heights.

His sergeant had appeared to him in the darkness, in the

cold miserable darkness, showing the whites of his eyes with his body tensed stiffly.

"My God, I saw him do it!"

"What?"

"With his own pistol."

"What—damn it!"

The sergeant led him back into a pine stand. Deneen was sitting beneath thick, dripping branches, huddled close to the tree trunk. His pistol was in his hand. And the toe of his right boot was missing—where he had shot it away.

They carried him to the rear and said *shrapnel* to the orderly who was filling out the tag which was attached to Deneen's tunic. The remainder of the night Flynn did not smile because he was muscle-tight in the mud as A. P. Hill's Whitworths continued to slam down from Hazel Grove.

In the morning he found the sergeant dead; killed in the shelling. And he realized he was the only one who knew about Deneen.

After that he smiled when he felt like smiling.

In the army it wasn't necessary. Most of the time it helped, but it wasn't necessary. He had seen men do more than just smile to wangle a post assignment back East. He had accepted this, regarding it as something contemptible, but still, none of his business. He had accepted this and all of the unmilitary facets of army life because there was nothing he could do about them. The politics could go their smiling, boot-licking way.

There had to be men on frontier station. There had to be men who took dirty assignments and made successes of them. And when he found himself in the role—when he found himself in a part of the army which still occasionally fought, he accepted it as quickly and as readily as the politics. Somebody had to do it. Do what you can do best. That's how to make a success. Even if the success is only a self-satisfaction.

But there was an end to it.

The beginning of the end was the day a Major Deneen suddenly appeared at Fort Thomas as Post Commandant.

He said nothing to Deneen about that night at Chancellorsville; and was shocked when one day he heard Deneen refer to his wound quite proudly. Others were present, but Deneen had looked directly at Flynn as he described it, the shelling, and the damn odd place to be caught by shrapnel. Flynn was certain, then, that Deneen had been in a state of shock and was not even slightly aware of what had happened that night.

Then, suddenly, Flynn found himself with unreasonable hastily planned assignments. He had had them before—all patrols were not routine—but now they began in earnest. Bold orders that were *cavalry,* but not the way to fight Apaches. Following sign blindly because Deneen insisted on speed. Wandering, ill-provisioned decoy patrols that whittled down his men. In seven months he had lost more men than any officer at Fort Thomas.

The end came during the Tonto campaign, almost a full year to the day since Deneen had arrived as post commander. They had chased Primero and his Tonto Apaches for five weeks and toward the end, when they knew they had the war chief and his small band, Deneen took the field. He arrived in the evening as three companies were closing in on Bosque Canyon in the Mogollon country. Primero was inside, somewhere among the shadowy rock formations.

And Deneen ordered Flynn to take half of B and gallop through the narrow passage in order to draw fire. That would tell them where the damn hostiles were!

"I suggest scouting first, sir."

"You suggest nothing."

"Madora's Coyotero scouts could belly in after dark and tell us exactly where they are."

"Are you refusing an order?"

He went in at dawn with fourteen men. Yes, they drew fire . . . and it was almost noon before they were pulled out. Six of them, Flynn with an arrow wound in his thigh.

Deneen was in the tent they had rigged for him. He was not present as they brought in what was left of B, and Flynn found him there alone.

"You're killing good men to get me."

Deneen said nothing.

"You knew what you were doing at Chancellorsville. I should have realized it before this. You're afraid of me because of what I know. You're afraid I'll tell others what a yellow son of a bitch of an excuse for a man you are!"

Calmly, quietly, "When we return to Thomas, Mr. Flynn, you will be confined to your quarters. At the moment, you are in need of the surgeon's attention."

He resigned shortly after that and never again referred to Chancellorsville in Deneen's or anyone else's presence. It would do little good to tell others. Some would believe him, most would not, and either way it would accomplish nothing. He resigned hastily; too hastily perhaps, and regretted it almost immediately.

He did the next best thing—in many respects, the better thing, as he came to know his job more thoroughly—he signed up as a contract guide. He could make his own calculations and patrol officers respected his opinion. He had learned from Joe Madora and that was good enough for most. Many of these officers were new to him, for he made sure he was not assigned to Fort Thomas. But after Deneen was appointed Department Adjutant, he did work out of Thomas for almost a year—seeing Deneen occasionally, seldom speaking to him—until he was assigned to the territorial prison at Yuma. Madora fought it because it was a sheer waste of Flynn's capabilities, but he could do nothing. The order had come from the office of the Department Adjutant.

He resigned again, this time breaking all ties, and went gold prospecting down into the Sierra Madre.

Now you're back, he thought, still watching the sky. Because this is what you like to do and you hoped Deneen might have forgotten. But nothing has changed. Deneen is still Deneen. It's something in his mind. You are the only living man who saw what happened that night at Chancellorsville, which seems so long ago; something he's trying to convince himself did not happen. As if by getting you out of his sight it will cease to have ever existed.

But now you're back and he's going to a lot of trouble to make you quit again. It must be very important to him. What did Madora say: You might be mad enough to do this just so you can throw it back in Deneen's face. Does that make sense? I don't know. But this time there's no quitting. The sooner he realizes it, the better. It will either straighten him out, or drive him crazier than he already is. But it is hard to feel sorry for him.

Four

●

Early afternoon of the third day, in high timbered country, they looked out over a yellow stretch of plain to see smoke rising from the hills beyond. It lifted lazily in a wavering thin column above the ragged hillcrests.

"From here," Bowers said, "it could even be a barbecue." He put his glasses on the spot and focused, clearing the haze, drawing the thin spire closer. He studied the land silently.

"Coming from a draw beyond that first row of hills," he said then. "I would say—two miles."

"Not much more," Flynn said. "A trail cuts through the trough of the hills directly across from us."

"What's there that will burn?"

"Nothing."

"A house?"

"Not unless it was built in the last six months. It would be a jacale—and brush houses don't burn that long."

"Well, maybe it's . . ." He would have said, A wagon or wagon train, but he stopped, remembering the Esteban family that Flynn had described to him being only a day or so ahead of them; and he felt suddenly self-conscious, as if

Flynn were reading his thoughts; and he said, "I don't know."

"You were going to say wagons, weren't you?"

Bowers nodded.

They had dismounted. Now they stepped into the saddles and nudged their mounts out of the timber diagonally down the slope that fell to the plain, and reaching the level they followed the base of the hill through head-high brush, keeping the plain on their left. They went on almost two miles until the plain began to crumble into depressions and the brush patches thickened, and when finally the flatness gave way to rockier ground they turned from the hill and moved across slowly so there would be no dust. They were beyond the smoke column, which had thinned, and now they doubled back more than a mile before climbing into timber again, following switchbacks single file as the hill rose steeper.

Near the crest, they tied their mounts and both drew Springfield carbines from the saddle boots.

Bowers lifted a holstered revolving pistol which hung from the saddle horn and secured it to the gun belt low on his hip. Watching him, Flynn's elbow tightened against his body to feel the heavy bulk of his own pistol beneath the coat.

"Ready?"

Bowers nodded and they moved up the remaining dozen yards of the hill, brushing the pine branches silently. At its crest the hill flattened into a narrow grove, thick with piñons. They passed through in a half-crouch and went down on hands and knees when the trees ended abruptly in a sandy slope that dropped before them more than a hundred feet. Below, the pines took up again, but here were taller and more thinly scattered. Through them, they could see patches of the trail which passed through the trough of the hill.

And directly below them, through a wide smooth-sand clearing, they saw the charred shapes of three wagons.

They were no longer wagons but retained some identity in a grotesque, blackened flimsiness; two of the wagons, their trees pointing skyward and only half burned, were rammed into the bed of the third which was over on its side. The mules had been cut from the traces and were not in sight.

Smoke from the suffocated fire hung like hot steam over the rubble of partly burned equipment—cooking gear, cases of provisions, clothing and bedding—heaped and draped about the wagons. The smoke was thinning to nothing above the wreckage, but its stench carried higher, even to the two men.

A bolt of red material, like a saber slash across the flesh-colored sand, trailed from a scorched end at one of the wagons to the base of a heavy-boled pine a few yards up the glade. And through the lower branches they saw the arm extended to clutch the end of the cloth. The arm of a woman.

A stillness clung to the narrow draw. Bowers heard a whispered slow-drawl of obscenity, but when he glanced at Flynn the scout's lean face was expressionless. He lay on his stomach looking down the short barrel of his carbine. Bowers nudged him and when Flynn glanced up the two men rose without a sound and started down the loose sand.

They came to the woman beneath the pine and Flynn parted the branches with the barrel of his carbine, then stooped quickly. Bowers saw the figure of a young girl, but Flynn was over her then and he could not see her face, though he glimpsed the sand dark with blood at her head.

Flynn came up slowly and said, "Anita Esteban's cousin," but he was thinking something else. It was in his eyes that looked past Bowers to the burned wagons. "Somebody took her hair," he said.

They separated, Flynn following the sand clearing, and came out on the trail a dozen yards apart. He looked uptrail toward Bowers, then felt his nerves jump as he saw the bodies off to the side of the road.

Two men and a young boy. Worn, white cotton twisted unnaturally. He could see the rope soles of their sandals. They lay face-down with the backs of their heads showing the blood-matted, scorched smear where they had been shot from a distance of no more than a yard. He moved toward Bowers and watched the lieutenant kneel beside another sprawled figure. As he drew closer, he saw that it was Anastacio Esteban.

Bowers looked up at him. "He's dead."

"They're all dead," Flynn said quietly. He looked past Bowers and saw other forms straggled along the side of the trail. Even from a distance he was certain they were dead. Then he knelt down next to Anastacio whom he had known a long time and he made the sign of the cross and said the Hail Mary slowly, for Anastacio and for the others.

Bowers looked at him curiously because he had not expected to see him pray, then motioned up the draw. "There are more up there." The other two wagons were roughly a hundred yards beyond and partly hidden by the brush where they stood off the trail.

He said to Flynn, "They had mules, didn't they?"

"They must have."

Flynn looked up-trail toward the two wagons. The animals that had pulled them were not in sight, but these wagons had not been burned. He heard Bowers say, "I hear 'Paches would rather eat a mule than even a horse."

In the shallow bed of the first wagon they found a woman with a child in her arms and next to her were two children clinging tightly to each other. No one was in the second wagon, but in the brush close by they found others. Most of them had been shot from close range.

Up beyond the second wagon they saw a woman lying in the middle of the trail. Her arms were spread with her fingers clawed into the loose sand. Flynn went to her quickly. Bowers watched him stoop over her then come up, shaking his head. Nita Esteban was not among the dead.

Flynn came back carrying the girl in his arms and placed her gently in the wagon. Bowers saw that she had been scalped; and his head turned to look at other things.

"They're changing their ways," Flynn said.

Bowers looked at him questioningly.

"Have you ever seen an Apache ambush?"

Bowers hesitated. "No."

"Well don't put this down as typical."

Bowers said, with embarrassment, "I'm sorry . . . about this."

"I knew Anastacio. The others I met only once."

Bowers looked up. "I thought you knew the girl well."

Flynn shook his head. "It only seems that way."

"They must have taken her."

"And perhaps others." Flynn was silent as his eyes went over the ambush—the burned wagons, the dead. "Mister, I'll tell you something. This isn't Apache."

"What other tribes are down here?"

"No other, to speak of."

"Well?"

"It isn't Indian."

"You're serious?"

"It was made to look Apache. And they did a poor job."

"I've heard that Apaches *are* known to kill."

"With bullets?"

"Why not?"

"Because they can't walk down to the corner and buy a box whenever they feel like it. Almost all the people were killed after they'd given up—*with bullets*—and that isn't Apache. On top of being hard to get, a bullet's too quick."

"I've been told not to try to figure them," Bowers said.

"That might apply to *why* they do something, but you can make sense out of how they do it." To Flynn the signs were plain. Many were plain because they were not there. A branch had been used to drag the footprints out of the sand. That wasn't Apache. The wasting of bullets. The scalping. Generally Apaches did not scalp. But they learn quickly. They have learned many things from the white man. They take the children of certain ages, to bring them up in the tribe because there was always a shortage of men. And there were many children here, dead, that an Apache would have taken.

They took Nita, and perhaps others, he thought. The taking of women is Apache—but it is hardly exclusively so.

And there were other things that he felt that told him this wasn't the work of Apaches. But it would take time to tell Bowers.

"Lieutenant," he said then. "You've got your work cut out for you. Get your tactical mind turning while I go up-trail."

Bowers began gathering the bodies, dragging them to a level sandy opening off the trail. His body was tense as he worked. He was aware of this, but he could not relax. He thought: They looked deader because their clothes are white —and because they were shot in the back of the head.

He looked up-trail, up the slight rise over which Flynn had disappeared, then to the high steep banks of the draw. A faint breeze moved through the narrowness; it brushed the pine branches lazily and carried the burned-wood smell of the wagons to the young lieutenant. The redheaded, sun-burned, slim-hipped lieutenant who had graduated fifteenth in his class from the Point and was granted his request for cavalry duty because of his high grades and because his father had been a brigadier general. His father was dead five months now. The smooth-faced, clean-featured, unsmiling lieutenant who now felt nervously alone with the dead and looked at the slopes, squinting up into the dark green, his eyes following the furrows of cream yellow that zigzagged up the crest; then, above the crest, the pale blue of the sky and the small specks that were circling lazily, gliding lower, waiting for the things that were alive to leave the things that were dead.

This was not cavalry. This was not duty his father, the brigadier, had described. A year at Whipple Barracks and he had not once worn his saber beyond the parade quadrangle. Four-day patrols hunting something that was seldom more than a flick of shadow against towering creviced walls of andesite. Patrols led by grizzled men in greasy buckskin who chewed tobacco and squinted into the sun and pointed and would seldom commit themselves. Cautious, light-sleeping men who moved slowly and looked part Indian. Every one of them did.

No, Flynn did not. That was one thing you could say for him. He was different from most of the guides; but that was because he had been an officer. One extreme, while the old one with the beard, Madora, was another. That was too bad about Madora, but perhaps he would recover. Flynn did not seem to view things in their proper perspective. He had probably been a slovenly officer. Deneen had said he would have to be watched, but he knows the country and that's what qualified him for this mission. Mission! Dragging home a filthy, runaway Indian who didn't know when he was well off. An unreasoning savage, an animal who would do a thing like this. Flynn is out of his mind thinking it was someone else. Get it over with. That's all; just get it over with.

When Flynn returned he was leading two mules.

"Those must have gotten away," Bowers said.

"Or else they didn't want them."

"Not if they were Apaches," Bowers said.

Flynn nodded. "That's right. Not if they were Apaches."

They hitched the mules to one of the wagons, binding the cut traces, and loaded the dead into the flat bed; they moved off slowly, following the draw that twisted narrowly before beginning a curving gradual climb that once more brought them to high open country. By noon of the next day they would be in Soyopa. They would bring the people home to be buried.

Later, as the trail descended, following the shoulder of the slope, Flynn studied the ribbon of trail far below. It would be dark before they reached the bottom, he knew. They both rode on the wagon box, their horses tied to the tailgate.

First he saw the dust. It hung in the distance, filtered red by the last of the sun. Whatever had raised it was out of sight now.

Then, below—small shapes moving out of shadow into

strips of faded sunlight—two riders, moving slowly, bringing up the rear of whatever was up ahead. The riders seemed close, but they were not within rifle range.

"Lieutenant, let me have your glasses."

There was something familiar about the rider on the left, even at this distance. Flynn put the glasses to his eyes and brought the riders close and there it was, as if looking into the future, seeing Frank Rellis riding along with the Winchester across his lap.

Five

●

Standing in the doorway, Lieutenant Lamas Duro scratched his bare stomach and smacked his lips disgustedly. The taste of mescal was stale in his mouth. A feeling of faintness came on him, then passed just as suddenly and left him wide awake. He swallowed again as his tongue searched the inside of his mouth. And finally Lieutenant Duro decided that he did not feel too badly considering the mescal and the few hours sleep. Perhaps the mescal had not worn off completely. That was it.

He looked at the corporal, who smiled at him showing bad teeth, and he thought: If he is as frightened as I know he is, why should he smile? Why should he curl his diseased mouth which makes me despise him all the more? He shrugged to himself as his hands felt the flatness of his pockets. Then he moved the few steps from the sleeping-room doorway into the front room, and drew a cigar from a packet on the cluttered desk.

The corporal, who was a small man, watched him with wide-open eyes and nervously fingered into his pocket for a match; but when he scratched it against the adobe wall it broke in his hand, unlighted.

Lieutenant Lamas Duro, chief of rurales, took a match from the desk, shaking his head faintly, and scratched it across the scarred surface of the desk. Holding it to the cigar, he looked at the corporal and the corporal's eyes shifted quickly from his own.

He moved his hand idly over the hair of his stomach and chest and the hint of an amused smile played about the corners of his sensitive mouth. The corporal, a cartridge bandoleer crossing his faded gray jacket, stood at a rigid but stoop-shouldered attention, his eyes focussed now somewhere beyond the lieutenant, seeing nothing.

"You have a good reason for hammering my door at this hour?" The lieutenant spoke calmly, yet his words seemed edged with a threat.

"Teniente, the execution," the corporal said with his eyes still on the wall beyond.

"What execution?"

"The Indian who was taken yesterday, Teniente. The one who accompanies the American."

"Oh . . ." There was disappointment in his voice.

The day before, an American had wandered into Soyopa with a glittering display of goods—kitchen utensils, cutlery, leather goods, hats, even suits of clothes. The boxes filled his Conestoga to such capacity that many of the pots and pans hung from racks along the sides. And with him was the Aravaipa Apache boy.

The boy was perhaps thirteen, certainly not older, but still an Apache. Lieutenant Duro's duty was to rid this territory of banditry, and this included Apaches. They were simple instructions with few qualifications. No exceptions. If the Apache was foolish enough to enter Soyopa, so be it. Let him make his grace with God. His scalp was worth one hundred pesos.

The trader was escorted far out of sight of the pueblo and sent on his way, after protests. The Territorial Commission would hear about this. But Lieutenant Duro could make no exceptions. It pained him that the villagers would have no opportunity to make purchases, but he must think of their protection and welfare first. He had told this to Hilario, the alcalde. Often the upholding of the law is unpleasant. One must often act against his heart.

"Why there are even things I wanted to buy," he told the alcalde, "but I could not." And while he said it, he thought of the law of compensation. The good are rewarded. He still had the Apache boy.

"Also, Teniente . . ."

"Yes!" He bellowed the word and glared, and now smiled only within himself, watching the frightened corporal. What excuses for men I have, he thought. What a magnificently stupid son of the great whore this one is.

"It is the alcalde. He desires to speak with you."

"What did you tell him?"

The corporal stammered, "I told him I would present his request."

"Have you presented it now?"

"Yes, Teniente."

"Then what keeps you here?" The corporal turned with an eagerness to be out, but Duro brought him up sharply. "Corporal!"

"Yes, Teniente."

"Corporal . . ." He spoke softly moving back toward the sleeping room, still idly rubbing his stomach, and nodded into the room. ". . . when you go, take that cow of a woman with you . . ."

The west wall of the courtyard was bullet-riddled from one end to the other, though the pockmarks were scattered at the extreme ends. Towards the center they were more clustered and in some few places the bullet holes formed gouges —scarred patches from which the adobe had crumbled, leaving hollows.

And it appeared that the wearing away of the wall was a concern of Sergeant Santana's. He varied the position of his riflemen with a calculated deliberateness which argued reason, moving them along the wall with each execution.

At one time, perhaps the appearance of the wall had been his concern, but it had become lost in routine; so that now he moved his riflemen back and forth simply because he was able to do so. He knew that bullets would never probe completely through the thick adobe—not in his lifetime; nor did he care if they ever would.

This morning, Sergeant Santana measured the paces from the line of six riflemen to the wall. He counted twelve in time with his strides, then raised the quirt which was attached to his wrist and waved it in an indolent, sweeping motion toward the rear door of the adobe building. He lighted a cigar, leisurely, and when he looked at the door again they were bringing out the Apache boy.

Walking into the yard now, two men in front of him, two behind and one on each side, he seemed very small. Pathetically small. Santana shrugged and blew smoke out slowly. An Apache was an Apache. He had heard even the teniente say that.

They placed him close to the wall where Santana indicated with his quirt, and a rurale remained on either side of him holding his arms, though his hands were tied behind his back. The others moved away to join the line of men along the back of the house.

Santana's eyes followed them then shifted to the back door, expecting it to open, but it remained closed and again he turned to the Apache who was looking about with little show of concern.

His trousers were too large, bunched at the waist and tucked into moccasins rolled beneath his knees. His shirt was dirty, faded blue, and only his moccasins and headband indicated that he was Apache. The two rurales, in their dove-gray uniforms and crossed bandoleers, were a half-head taller than the boy who would move his chin from one shoulder to the other to look at them, studying the leather cartridge belts and the silver buttons on the soft gray jackets.

And all about the courtyard were these men with their guns and so many bullets that they must have special belts to hang them over their shoulders. The boy was aware that he was going to die, but there were so many things of interest to see. He hoped they might delay it for a little while longer.

Two Americans came in through the gateway in the east wall. They strolled leisurely, smoking cigarettes, and as they approached Santana one of them called, "You better get closer, that boy's kinda small."

Both of them laughed, but Santana ignored them and looked toward the house's rear door.

They were gaunt-faced men, both needed a shave, and they wore their hats low on their foreheads against the morning sun. They stood with their thumbs in low-slung gun belts watching Santana and the rifleman. Now the one who had spoken before said, "Hey, Santy! We'll lay you even, three of the six don't hit the boy!"

They grinned, waiting for the sergeant to answer. Santana said with contempt, "Listen to the great killers of Indians."

One of the Americans said, "Well?" but Santana had turned his back to them.

Through the gateway now came a group of men dressed in white peon clothes and straw sombreros. There were six in all, but five of them walked close together, a few strides behind the older man with the bronzed face and white mustache. Hilario Esteban, the alcalde of Soyopa, walked with more dignity than the others who seemed purposely holding back, as if reluctant to enter the courtyard.

And at that moment, Lieutenant Duro came out of the back door of the adobe building. He was hatless, his jacket open, and a white scarf draped loosely about his neck. A cigar was in the corner of his mouth. Drawing on it, he glanced at Hilario Esteban who was only a few paces away. But when he saw the old man about to speak, he turned his head quickly toward Santana who was coming over from the rifle squad.

Lieutenant Duro then looked about the courtyard leisurely, from the riflemen to the Apache, then to the two Americans and the rest of his rurales in the narrow shade of the house. He ignored Hilario and his delegation of villagers. He was sick of their wide-eyed hesitancy, their halfhearted pleading on matters of no importance as they twisted the brims of their sombreros with nervous fingers. Hilario was different, he admitted to himself. But he was of the other extreme. Hilario had been with Juarez at Querétaro and had witnessed the execution of Maximilian and he retained strange ideas concerning rights. Hilario would have to be shown his place.

Santana stood before him now, idly slapping the quirt against the booted calf of his leg. Lieutenant Duro eyed the cigar in the sergeant's mouth. He took a long, sucking draw on his own then dropped it to the ground. He looked directly at the sergeant, exhaling the smoke slowly.

The sound of the quirt slapping against leather stopped.

Santana returned the lieutenant's stare, his cigar clenched in the corner of his mouth, but only for a moment. He dropped the cigar and ground it into the hard-packed sand.

Duro smiled faintly. "We are ready now?" he said.

Santana mumbled, "Ready," and turned to go back to the firing squad.

"Sergeant!"

Santana turned slowly.

"Listen. Ask your marksmen to aim lower than the head."

"Yes, Teniente."

"And take his hair neatly when it is over."

Santana nodded toward the two Americans who were watching with interest. "Perhaps one of those should do that."

Duro smiled again. "You would debate the matter?"

"I was only talking."

"Talk to your marksmen," Lieutenant Duro said.

As Santana moved off, Hilario Esteban approached Duro. "May I ask a question, Señor Duro?"

The Lieutenant's eyes followed Santana. "What is it?"

"I would ask by what right you kill this Apache boy."

"You answer your own question. He is Apache."

"He is a peaceful Apache. The American merchant told us that he is Aravaipa, which have seldom been at war, and when they were, it was long ago. Besides, he is only a boy."

Duro looked at him with his faint smile. "Boys grow into men. Let's call these bullets the ounces of prevention."

"Señor Duro, this American will go back and tell his government . . ."

"What, that we have shot an Apache?"

Hilario shook his head and the lines of age in his face seemed more deeply etched. "Señor Duro, this one is at peace. He assists in the selling of the merchant's wares and entertains no thoughts common to the Apache. The American will tell his government what we have done and there will be ill feeling."

"Ill feeling! Old man, stop . . ."

"Señor, I am responsible for the welfare of travelers who visit Soyopa as well as our own people. I have a trust . . ."

"Do you really believe that?" Duro looked at the old man closely.

"With all certainty."

"You believe your office to be one of honor, which involves the bearing of grave responsibilities?"

"Señor Duro." Hilario's tone lost respect. "We are discussing the life of a boy. One who has done nothing hostile to any of us!"

"You actually believe the alcalde resides in a seat of honor?" The lieutenant's voice remained calm.

"Señor Duro . . ."

The lieutenant interrupted him. "Corporal!" And as the corporal hurried toward him, he said, "Since your office is of such magnitude, perhaps you should remain close to it. Sit at your desk, Alcalde, in your seat of honor, and contemplate your grave responsibilities." And then to the corporal, "Take your men and escort our alcalde to his office . . . and Corporal . . . if he puts his head out of the door . . . shoot him."

He waited until they had taken Hilario out of the courtyard—a rurale on each arm and others behind with their rifles at ready—the five of the peon delegation hurrying out ahead of them. Then he turned back to the firing squad. Santana was looking toward the gateway.

"Sergeant!" the lieutenant called, just loud enough to be heard. "If you please . . ." And he thought to himself: Lamas, you are an animal. But his mind shrugged it off, because it was a long way to Mexico City, and now he watched intently as the squad raised their rifles.

The two rurales moved away from the Apache boy. His eyes followed one of them as the dove-gray uniform moved off toward the house. The bullets go even all the way down the back! He heard a command in Spanish. One word. And there are so many of them; each man has two belts, and who knows, there might even be more stored in that great jacale. Another Spanish word broke the sudden stillness of the courtyard. Would it not be fine to have a belt with so many bullets. He heard the last command clearly . . . "Fire!"

Hilario Esteban, crossing the square, passing the slender obelisk of stone, heard the rifle fire. A short roll, a sharp, high-pitched echo that carried away to nothing. His shoulders hunched as if by reflex, then relaxed, and he sighed. A rifle barrel jabbed against his spine and only then did he realize that he had hesitated.

Six

●

Lieutenant Duro strolled through the east gate and circled the two-story building which served as his headquarters. It had been some-one's home when he arrived in Soyopa, but he'd forgotten whose now. On the lower floor he kept supplies—equipment, ammunition, spare rifles, all those things needed by his rurales. At the front, a stairway at each end of the ramada climbed to the floor above. This he had chosen for his living quarters. The two rooms were drab —bare, colorless adobe and board flooring that squeaked with each step. The quarters reminded Duro of the cell of a penitent monk; but in Soyopa what could one expect.

Two of his men stood in the shade of the ramada, guarding the possessions of the frontier police. They nodded as he rounded the building and straightened slightly, though their backs remained comfortably against the wall.

Duro shook his head wearily. What excuse for men, he thought. For months he had drilled, cursed and punished them into being soldiers; but it had been to no avail and now Lieutenant Duro was past caring. What did it really matter?

Mexico City was in another world, a hazy world that was becoming increasingly more difficult to conjure in his mind. He would picture himself as he had been at the Academy—and the bailes and the young girls who could not keep their eyes from the uniforms. But that had been during the short presidency of Don Sebastian Lerdo de Tejada. A few years seemed so long ago.

It was said often that the son of Don Agostino Duro, who was a personal friend of Lerdo Tejada, would rise from the Cadet Corps like a comet to a glorious career in the Army. When he received his lieutenancy, at the head of his class, Lamas Duro appeared well on the way. Unfortunately, Porfirio Diaz's political coup followed three months later.

Many of the Lerdistas disappeared, including Don Agostino Duro. His son, however, was a political enemy by blood, not by avocation; so Lamas disappeared merely from the capitol. His military training was something which could be utilized in Porfirio Diaz's new creation—the Rurales. The Frontier Police. And Soyopa was far enough from Mexico City to guard against Lamas Duro's blood interfering with his politics.

He gazed about the square now, motionless in the sunlight. Wind-scarred adobe, squat dwellings, most of them without ramadas, old looking beyond their years. The church was directly across from his headquarters—it rose sand-colored, blending with the surrounding buildings which pushed close to it, a wide door, but a belfry that was too low for the width of the building and it only vaguely resembled a church. Santo Thomás de Aquín.

Past the empty fountain with its solitary stone obelisk, Duro could see down a side street to the house of Hilario Esteban, and the two rurales lounging in the doorway. God in Heaven, how can I be given such men! He turned disgustedly then and climbed the stairs to the upstairs veranda. Before going inside, he looked out over the square again. But nothing had changed.

Curt Lazair remained in the lieutenant's chair as Duro entered from the veranda. He lounged comfortably with a boot hooked on the desk corner next to his hat and he eyed

Duro curiously. The rurale lieutenant had not seen him and was still deep in thought as he closed the door; and now Lazair smiled faintly.

"It's a long way to Mexico City."

Duro was startled. He turned from the door quickly and looked at the man with astonishment.

"Well, it's no farther than Anton Chico, New Mexico," Lazair went on. "Only Anton Chico ain't a hell of a lot better than Soyopa. It's all in how you look at things."

Duro nodded. "Yes, it's all in how you look at it." His head indicated the outside. "And I cannot say that I see very much out there."

Lazair smiled again—a smile which said he believed in little and trusted in even less. He shrugged now and said, "Money."

There was little sense in talking about it. Duro had discovered that the least said to this man, the better. Nothing seemed important to him. And always he was relaxed, as if to catch you unaware and then make fun of something which should be spoken of with sincerity. He wants to make you mad, Duro thought. Tell him to go to hell. But instead, he said, quietly, "You need a shave."

"I been out working for you." Lazair passed the palm of his hand over dark, neatly combed hair. "But I slicked my hair down when I found out I had to visit the lieutenant," he said mockingly. He was a man close to forty, almost handsome, crudely handsome, and the glistening hair contrasted oddly with the beard stubble on his face. He wore soft leather pants tucked into his boots; pistols on both sides of his low-slung cartridge belt, and he slipped one of the pair up and down in the holster idly as he spoke.

His other hand dropped from the arm of the chair now and he lifted a canvas bag and swung it onto the table.

"I brought you something."

Duro made no move toward the desk, though his eyes fell on the bag. "How many women did you kill this time?"

The words had no visible effect on Lazair. "Count 'em and see."

"I'll take your word for the number. I trust though you've taken the ribbons from the hair," Duro said.

Lazair nodded. "Sure we did. Just like you wiped that little boy's nose before you shot him a while ago."

"Were you there?"

"Two of my men were. I just come in."

"You're quickly informed."

Lazair smiled. "You got to get up a hell of a lot earlier than you do."

"How many did you take?" Duro said irritably. "I don't have all day."

"Open it up and find out."

"I said I'd take your word!"

Lazair came off the chair then and pulled the sack toward him. As he untied the rawhide string he said, "You're awful goddamn squeamish about something you're making money out of."

Duro said nothing as Lazair opened the bag and held it upside-down. The scalps came out of the bag as one—a hairy mass, glistening black and matted with dried blood. Duro frowned as Lazair ran his hand through the pile, separating the scalps.

He said, "When did you take them?"

Lazair glanced at him as he lined the scalps along the edge of the desk. "What difference does it make?"

"They smell."

Lazair laughed out. "Man, these used to be the tops of heads. What do you expect!"

"Put them back. I said I'd take your word for the number!"

But Lazair would not be hurried. "Even salted 'em down." He looked up at the lieutenant then and winked. "After I greased 'em good so they'd be sure and look Indian."

Duro studied the bounty hunter silently. Within him he could feel the hatred for this man. It caused a heat over his face. But he was aware of his conscience ever more than the hate, and he said very simply, "You are the filthiest man I have known."

"But you can't get really mad, can you?" Lazair said. "Not without hurting yourself. Daylight's a bad time of the day. It shows everything plain and if you happen to look in a mirror, you even see yourself." Lazair smiled again. "But there's always night . . . and your mescal bottle. . . . Just remember one thing, soldier boy, I don't need you as bad as you think I do. If I can buy you, then there's some other goddam broken-down soldier who'll act just as dumb for money you don't have to work for."

"Maybe you had better look for this other 'broken-down soldier'!" Duro flared.

Lazair shook his head, smilingly. "I don't have to. I know you too well. You're stuck here and you don't have a choice. And every year you see government pesos coming in for the scalp bounties. Easy money to take, it looks like, only you have to balance what goes out with a scalp coming in. But when somebody comes along and offers you money in return for taking *all* scalps—no questions—then you're just doing your job. All you got to do is add and subtract . . . and you know how to do that."

Duro said, "Add scalps that are not always Apache."

"It's up to you." Lazair shrugged. "If you want to quit vouching for 'em it's up to you. Only I don't think you can. You get back ten pesos for every hundred going out. That's a lot of mescal when all you got to do is add up when the government man comes around. He isn't going to feel 'em for texture. So don't give me any goddamn talk about keeping your hands clean, because they're just as dirty as mine. Maybe dirtier," Lazair said evenly, " 'cause I don't particularly like Mexicans anyway."

"Get out!" Duro screamed.

Lazair lifted his hat from the desk. "I wouldn't want to be in your skin. You don't know who to be mad at, do you?" He went to the door, then hesitated after he had opened it. "I know there's eight hundred pesos' worth there, so let's not go juggling the books. We'll settle after you've cooled off."

Duro waited until he heard Lazair descending the stairs. He went to the desk quickly then and began sweeping the scalps into the sack that he held open below the desk edge. As he did this, he did not look down and he brushed his hand stiffly, with the fingers held tightly together so that he would not feel their texture. Yet a picture formed in his mind. A picture with the shock of a knife thrust to the stomach . . . even though it was only an almost indiscernible Mexican woman, no one he recognized, but with flowing black hair . . .

Hilario Esteban had moved the stool close to the window so that he could look out into the street. The street seemed so deserted this morning. At first he thought it strange, then one of the rurales appeared near the window and it was not strange. There was little for these frontier soldiers to do, most of them stationed far from their own villages, and often their minds would be suddenly activated by the sight of a villager passing along the street.

And as if they were a breed apart and all others were enemies, they would do unnatural things. Hilario had seen them shoot at the heels of old women to cause them to run. It was a sight to see an old woman running, then fall—they always fell—and scramble and roll in the dust shrieking. And they would think of other things to while away the hours. Sometimes they were as children. Like the morning Hilario had awakened to find the obscene word painted on the front of his house. Four red letters reaching higher than a man's head. It had taken a full day's labor to scrape the paint from the adobe, and they had stood around to laugh as the alcalde performed such work.

He leaned out of the window now and looked to the side. The two pairs of legs extended from his door stoop. The front of the brim of a sombrero showed also, but that was all he could see. Maybe they were asleep now, he thought.

"God, make them sleep well and keep thoughts from their heads," he whispered.

They would not let him approach the door and earlier they had threatened him with the butts of their rifles when he wanted to open it. The house was becoming an oven and it was not good to remain in it with the door closed. Thankfully, he had the window—not all houses had a window—but he was used to having the door open. Perhaps it is better that it does remain closed, he thought. Else they might be tempted to enter and take something. Something of Nita's. Before, one of them had asked him where Nita was, then laughed and said something obscene. "God, why do you make such as these?" And then he thought: But if there were no evil men, then how could you tell the good? He pictured his wife then, for a reason he did not know, and he was glad that she was not here to witness his being degraded. Though she would understand. Maybe she sees anyway; but she is probably talking to the saints. He thought then of Francis of Assisi because he had been a very humble man, and he wondered what St. Francis would have done had he lived in Soyopa.

St. Francis would have pleaded for the life of the Apache boy. I know that, Hilario Esteban thought. But what can be done with a man like Lamas Duro, who is in such agony with his fate that he directs his anger to those beneath him?

In the beginning, Hilario had prayed for Duro's soul. He had felt honest sorrow for him. Now his prayers were less frequent. It was easy to despise Duro, but hard not to be afraid of him. Still, he opposed Duro because his conscience directed him to. A man cannot disobey his conscience. Perhaps when Anastacio returns things will be better. It is very lonely here without Nita, he thought.

Across the narrow street, on the wall that joined Anastacio's house, a faded poster advertised a bullfight in Hermosillo. Anastacio loved the Corrida, and had posted the sheet there more than a month ago. On their way to Willcox for a reunion, he had planned to stop in Hermosillo and take the entire family to the Corrida.

From the window, Hilaro read the poster again. How many times have I read that? he thought. I can see it in my mind clearly. Even that which I cannot read now. The lower part is torn, but it said at one time: *Sombra—3 pesos . . . Sol—1 peso. Boletos de venta en todas partes.*

He wondered then if Anastacio had taken enough money. How much . . . three pesos times eighteen . . . so that the family could reach the Corrida from the shade. He went into the rear room then to lie down. There was nothing more to see on the street.

One of the rurales awakened at the sound of the horses, but the other remained asleep, propped against the door. He opened his eyes to see the two Americans astride the horses, looking down at him and he nudged his companion awake as he heard one of the Americans ask, "This is the house of the alcalde, isn't it?"

The rurale nodded, but did not rise.

Flynn swung down then and approached the door. "What are you, the guard of honor?"

The rurale grinned at his companion and then toward Flynn. "More the guard of dishonor," he said.

"Where is the alcalde?"

"Within."

"Would you move, so I can knock on the door?"

"No one enters," the rurale said, rising. He held his rifle diagonally across his chest. His companion rose then. "Nor does the alcalde leave."

Flynn felt a sudden anger, but he waited until it passed. "Why?" he said.

"Because the teniente orders it!" the rurale said angrily.

"What did the alcalde do?"

The rurale smiled lazily at Flynn. "You ask many questions." He glanced at his companion who moved up next to him. "He asks many questions, doesn't he?" Then to Flynn he said, "Are you another of the great hunters of Apaches? Soyopa is honored." He bowed mockingly. His companion grinned, but he moved uneasily.

Flynn studied the two rurales. Crossed bandoleers over the gray uniforms that were worn slovenly. Shirts open at the throat and wide-brimmed sombreros off their foreheads. The one stood with his hip cocked and fingered his rifle eagerly. The other was not so sure of himself; it was apparent.

"I'm going to ask you one more question," Flynn said. He unbuttoned his coat and opened it enough to show the butt of his pistol. "Are you going to get out of the way?"

For a moment the rurale only stared. Then his elbow touched his companion's arm. "Perhaps this is something for the teniente. Bring him!" He glanced after his companion as he moved off hurriedly, then back to Flynn. "Man," he said, "your pistol is not as large as you think it is."

Hilario Esteban saw the rurale pass the window, beginning to run. He looked out now, frowning, as he heard someone speak, then his entire face wrinkled into a smile.

"Señor Flín!"

The rurale was startled. He brought the rifle around abruptly. Flynn's head turned, but there was another movement close to his chest. And abruptly the rurale's eyes widened and his face muscles went slack. First he felt the barrel press into his side, then the click of the hammer.

Close to his ear, Flynn said, "You're all through, soldier. Drop the rifle and go sit down."

Hilario disappeared from the window, but the door opened almost immediately and he was standing before them. "Davíd!" His face beaming. "What a day this is! When did you arrive?" He saw the pistol then and the smile left his face.

"It's all right, Hilario," Flynn said. "He didn't know we were friends." He glanced at Bowers who was holding their horses. "Hilario Esteban, this is Lieutenant Bowers."

Bowers said something in a low voice and he looked at Hilario embarrassedly.

Flynn looked at Bowers curiously. Then it came to him. You forgot! he thought. How in hell could you forget! As they rode in he had been ready. Preparing himself all morning as he listened to the creaking of the wagon wheels. Now he felt suddenly self-conscious, as if Hilario was already reading it in his face.

He heard Bowers say quietly, "Why don't you two go inside and talk things over."

Flynn wanted to tell him now, quickly, with Bowers there, but the presence of the rurale bothered him oddly. "Maybe we'd better," he said.

Hilario stepped back to let Flynn enter first, his gaze following the scout with a frowning, puzzled expression. Bowers had not moved his position, but now he lifted his pistol and turned it on the rurale as the two men passed into the room.

Once, Flynn rode into Fort Thomas with four men straggling behind him. Four returning out of twelve . . . and one of the eight dead was the patrol officer; so Flynn made the report. "Major"—it had not been Deneen then—"there are eight men back there in a draw, being hacked to pieces right now, because a wet-nosed lieutenant wanted to see how fast he could make a brevet." He told it bluntly because he was angry. The major knew he was sorry—sorry for the men, and sorry because the lieutenant wasn't there to learn a lesson. And after that, young officers fresh from the Point listened to him before entering quiet, peaceful-appearing draws. The major saw to that.

Another time he listened to an officer tell a woman that her husband did not return with the patrol. He listened to the man hesitate and falter and say "I'm sorry . . ." more than a dozen times. But none of the I'm-sorrys did any good. The woman went on crying with her shoulders quivering and her mouth twisted pathetically. The two children in the next room cried because they had never heard their mother do this before.

Another time. Another soldier's wife. She waited until they left before breaking down. While he and the major were there, she cried only within, but only a little, because she was still telling herself that it could not be true.

Flynn started at the beginning, telling Hilario about missing the family in Contention. He told him everything, each detail, speaking the words quietly without hesitating. And he watched Hilario's face change—from a smile at first to a dumb stare, an expression that meant nothing. He listed those they had brought back in the wagon, painfully aware of what his words were doing to the old man; but there was no other way. He told him that it had been Apaches—because there was no sense in going into the other now—and there was a chance Nita was still alive. He didn't say maybe it would be better if she were dead. And finally, when he had finished, he said the inevitable, "I'm sorry"—for what it was worth. He thought it might be easier to tell a man, but it was the same.

Hilario did not cry. He sat staring with nothing in his eyes, telling himself that it was not true. Picturing them alive, because he didn't know how to picture them dead.

Flynn stood near the window, waiting for the old man to speak. He wanted to say again that he was sorry and he tried to think of other ways to say it; but all the words were without substance, and probably the old man would not even hear them. He looked across to the poster which advertised the bullfight in Hermosillo.

PLAZA DE TOROS

HERMOSILLO

Mañana a las 4

Tres Grandes Toreros en Competencia

VIRAMONTES (Español)

vs.

Juan Toyas y Sinaloa (Mexicanos)

Seis Hermosos Toros

De la Famosa Ganadería de don Feliz Montoya

Precios de Entrada

From there down, the poster was torn from the wall.

Flynn felt the old man next to him then.

"The part that is not there," the old man said, "tells that it would cost three pesos to sit in the shade and one peso to sit on the side of the sun."

"I was looking at it . . ."

"I hope they were able to sit in the shade." He considered this silently. Then he said, "Where are they now?"

"We left the wagon back of the church, by the graves. There's a boy watching it." Flynn hesitated. He continued in Spanish, softly, "I think we should bury them soon, Hilario."

Hilario nodded, dazedly. "Yes. I will get the priest on the way."

"Flynn!"

He went to the door quickly. Bowers glanced at him, then beckoned up the street where it led into the square. "You better get out of here!"

"Are they coming?"

"The whole Mexican Army!"

Seven

●

A dozen horsemen swung onto the square from the street siding Duro's headquarters and crossed the open area, separating at the four-sided stone shaft, bunching again to enter the narrow street with a cloud of dust billowing after them.

They swung down, all of them except Sergeant Santana, and spaced out in a ragged line along the front of the house, eager for something to happen. Just the two Americans could not offer much resistance.

From the saddle, Santana glared at the rurale who had been on guard. "Pick up your rifle!"

"I was overpowered . . ."

"Pick up your rifle!"

Flynn felt the anger return, thinking of Hilario, and now these grinning animals to make a difficult situation worse. And even though he knew they couldn't be aware of Hilario's sorrow, still their presence grated against his nerves and polite explanation wouldn't do. The rifle was in the road a few feet from the door stoop. Flynn moved to it now and placed his boot on the barrel before the rurale could reach it.

"You can order your man wherever you like,"

he said to Santana, "but if he stays here he doesn't need the rifle."

"Your position is not the best for suggesting orders," Santana said, half-smiling. "What is this supposed to be, an exhibition of Señor Lazair's influence? If it is, go and tell him that I am not the teniente. I order my men with my own mind."

Flynn looked at him curiously. "I don't know this Lazair," he said.

"Come now, why else would you be here? The teniente proves to the alcalde that he is governing body of Soyopa, then the hunter of Indians must prove that his power over-bears the office of the teniente."

"Your words are nothing."

"Tell your leader," Santana said, "and he will explain it to you."

"Soldier, I'm not going to stand here and argue with you. If you want to order your men, order them some place else."

Santana moved his sombrero back from his forehead and looked at Flynn with amazement. "God in Heaven—how this one talks!"

From the doorway where he had been standing, Hilario moved to Flynn's side. "Señor Santana, these men do not belong to Lazair. This one I have known before, and the other is his good friend. They have come to see me."

"Many days on horseback just to see the poor alcalde of Soyopa?"

"They have come to tell me of the death of my family," Hilario said quietly.

Santana hesitated. "Your family?"

"They were killed by the Apaches as they returned home." Hilario's lips moved stiffly as he spoke the words and tried to picture what had taken place. He added, "These friends have brought them home to be buried."

"Your entire family—brothers, sisters, children?"

"I have not yet made a count."

Santana was silent for a long moment. Finally he shrugged

—what can one do?—and said wearily, "Tend to your dead, old man."

He guided his horse to a turn and his rurales swung into their saddles on the signal. Let the old man alone, he thought. Along with his dead. They will guard him for the time. He pressed his heels into the horse's sides and looked up toward the square, then reined in abruptly. Lieutenant Duro was entering the street.

He approached slowly, holding his mount to a walk, and passed through the rurales, making them pull their horses out of the way. He dismounted with the same slow deliberateness.

"Leaving?" he said to Santana.

"There is nothing to be done here."

"Am I the last to know when my orders are disobeyed?"

Santana dismounted reluctantly. "I did not wish to disturb you."

"From what!"

"Your own affairs."

"Perhaps I should judge that." He looked at Flynn and then to Bowers. "What do you want here!"

"We've already done all the explaining we're going to do," Flynn said shortly.

"Hilario Esteban's family has been killed by the Apaches," Santana said bluntly. "These came to tell him of it."

"Oh. . . ." Duro's expression eased. Instinctively he said, "May I express my deep sympathy." To Flynn he said, "Did it occur near here?"

"Yesterday afternoon. About ten hours ride in the wagon."

"Oh. . . . You were on your way to Soyopa?" And when Flynn nodded, Duro said, "Perhaps on business?"

Flynn said, "You might say that." The lieutenant irritated him strangely. All of a sudden he was too friendly.

"We hope your stay in Soyopa will be a pleasant one," Lieutenant Duro said. He had already forgotten about the alcalde's family. Here was something to wonder about. Two more bounty hunters? Perhaps. And perhaps not. "We are at your service, señor . . . ?"

"Flynn. My friend's name is Bowers."

"It is a pleasure," Duro said, bowing slightly. "Perhaps you would find the time to dine with me later in the day."

Flynn glanced at Hilario. "Perhaps another time."

"Certainly . . . another time. And Hilario, if there is anything my men can do to assist you . . ."

The old man looked at the lieutenant with disbelief.

The man at the corner flicked his cigarette into the street and turned away, walking back down the row of adobe building fronts to the mescal shop. It was in the middle of the block on this, the west side of the square. A sign above the door said, Las Quince Letras—red lettering crudely done and fading as the adobe sand wore away. The man opened the screen door and put his head inside.

"Warren!"

He heard the horses behind him then and let the door swing closed and turned to see the rurales crossing the square at a trot. He watched Duro dismount in front of his headquarters and climb the stairs as his rurales passed down the side street. They would be returning to their garrison of tents on the south side of the village. Duro kept only two men with him on guard duty.

The one called Warren came out of the mescal shop adjusting his hat, squinting in the direction the rurales had gone. "They going home?"

The two men were the Americans who had witnessed the execution that morning. Now the one who had been on the corner, whose name was Lew Embree, said, "They let them go. They're not even guarding the old man any more."

"Who do you suppose they are?"

"I don't know," Lew said.

"Maybe we ought to tell Lazair," Warren said.

They looked up as Flynn and Bowers and Hilario Esteban came out of the street and crossed to the church, following the church yard back to the house in which the priest lived. The cemetery was just beyond. The two men watched them pass out of sight.

Warren said, "All of a sudden the old man can go where he wants." He tried to understand this. "Maybe Duro feels sorry for him."

"Or else he's tiptoeing till he finds out what's going on," Lew Embree said. "That younger one's got army written all over him, but that doesn't mean anything. He might of just gotten out." He shrugged. "We'll let Lazair figure it out."

They rode out of Soyopa by the south road, passing the rurales' camp area, and went on in the same direction for almost three miles before beginning a gradual swing to the east. Hours later, toward evening, they were traveling northeast and now began a winding, gradual climb into timber, scrub oak at first then cedar and sycamores and finally, when they were up high, pines. They crossed a meadow of coarse sabaneta grass and as they approached the heights on the west side, the sun barely showed over the rim-rock.

The base of the slanting rock wall was in deep shadow, and passing into the dimness, Warren said, looking up overhead, "Somebody must be asleep."

They heard the *click* close above them, sharp in the stillness—the lever action of a carbine. "Stand there!"

Lew looked up, but could not see the guard. "Who's that, Wesley?" He called out, "Wes, it's me and Warren!"

The voice answered, "What're you sneaking up for?—sing out, or you're liable to get shot!"

"Go to hell. . . ."

They passed on, entering a defile that climbed narrowly before opening again on a pocket in the rocks, walled on all sides. Four tents formed a semicircle behind a cook fire. Off to the left another fire glowed in the dusk, a smaller one, in front of a tarpaulin rigged over the entrance to a cave. The cave was Curt Lazair's. His fourteen men shared the tents.

Lew Embree handed his reins to Warren who led their horses off to where the others were picketed along the far right wall. He nodded to the men sitting around the cook fire. They looked up from tin plates, some mumbling hello, and watched him make his way over to the cave, wondering what had brought him from the pueblo, and as he reached the tarpaulin awning, Curt Lazair appeared in the entrance.

"What are you doing back?"

"Somebody hauled in a load of dead Mexicans right after you left," Lew said.

"I didn't think they'd find 'em so quick." Lazair eased into a camp chair, sucking his teeth, and propped his feet on a saddle in front of the chair. "You eaten yet?"

"No."

Lazair nodded back toward the cave entrance. "That girl ain't a bad cook . . . At least she's good for something."

"The people who found 'em weren't from Soyopa."

Lazair looked up. "Who were they?"

"A couple of Americans."

"Prospectors?"

Lew shrugged. "That's the question nobody knows."

"Well, why didn't you stay to find out?"

"I figured you'd want to know right away."

"You could've left Warren there."

"Between the mescal and that saloon whore he'd find out a hell of a lot."

"What'd they look like?"

"Like anybody else." Lew shrugged. "They weren't carrying signs."

"What!"

Lew reconsidered. "One of them looked army."

"A lot of people were in the army. What does that look like?"

"He had an army pistol holster on him . . ."

"You're about as much good as Warren."

"What did you want me to do, go up and ask 'em for their cards?"

"There're enough rum-bum rurales you could have asked!"

"How would they know?"

"Because they live in Soyopa and talk to people . . . those two aren't bringing the bodies into Soyopa 'cause they don't know anybody here! Why didn't they haul them to Rueda or Alaejos? They're just as close."

"Oh. . . ."

"Oh," Lazair mimicked him. He rolled a cigarette then, idly, considering what this could mean.

Lew said, "Maybe we shouldn't of hit that wagon string. There were too many of 'em . . . all from Soyopa."

Lazair said nothing.

"Now," Lew went on, "people right in the village have got kin and close friends to pray over and wonder about . . . and maybe they'll wonder so long they'll figure something out."

"How much they hate the Apaches," Lazair said. "That's all the figuring they'll do."

"I don't like it."

"I didn't ask you to like it! You don't get paid for your smiles!"

"Maybe those two Americans'll figure out something . . ."

"Goddamn it shut up, will you! I can't think with you crying in my ear!"

Two Americans suddenly appear with the bodies. They must have had a reason for coming down here. They stumble onto the ambush and know exactly where to cart the bodies; they knew they were from Soyopa, Lazair thought. Hell, if they knew where they were from, then they knew who they were! Why? Maybe one of the Mexicans had something on him that told what his village was. What are you getting so excited about? Probably a couple of saddle tramps looking for greener grass. Just mustered out of the Army. Maybe they heard about the scalp bounty and thought it was worth a try. You son of a bitch, you've got fourteen men with you and you worry about two. But all of a sudden people were starting to pop out of nowhere. Like the man they ran into just before the ambush *who wanted to join* the band. Well, the ambush was his test. He came out all right. If he had backed down, he'd have been left with the dead. Sure, he turned out all right. He thought now: And maybe he saw them. He must have come down the same way.

He called over to the cook fire, "Frank!"

The man was a shadowy figure crossing the camp area, taking his time until finally he appeared out of the dimness in front of the fire at the edge of the tarp awning. Frank Rellis had changed little. Dirtier, that was all.

"What?"

"When you were coming down from Contention, did you see anybody?"

"Did I see anybody?"

"Two Americans."

"What the hell kind of a question is that?" Rellis said.

Lazair swung on Lew irritably. "What did they look like!"

"One was a little taller than medium size, thin in the hips and put his boots down hard like a horse soldier. A young fella with red hair. The other one had a mustache, light-colored. He was stringier than the other fella and seemed taller. He looked peaceful enough, but his coat bulged a little like he had a six-gun under it."

Rellis said instantly, "A soldier mustache?"

Lew said, "Yeah, and the other one had an army holster on his side."

"Where are they?"

Lazair looked at Rellis curiously. "You know them?"

"Where are they?"

"Soyopa. They found those dead Mexicans and brought 'em in," Lazair said watching him closely. "I asked you if you knew them."

"I don't know. Maybe I do. One of them sounds like an old friend. Maybe I ought to go to Soyopa and find out for sure." He walked away before Lazair could ask him anything else.

Lazair watched him go back to the cook fire. The hell with

it, he thought. Getting anything out of that son of a bitch is like pulling teeth. If it was something to worry about he would have said something. He looked at Lew Embree. "You want a drink?"

"Fine."

Lazair half turned and called behind him, "Honey!" There was no answer and he winked at Lew. "She's bashful."

Lew grinned, rubbing the back of his hand across his mouth. "How is she?"

"I can't even get her to smile."

"They don't have to smile."

"Honey!" Lazair called again. "Bring us out a bottle of something!"

Nita Esteban appeared in the cave opening, in half-shadow, the light of the fire barely reaching her. She held the ends of a red scarf that was about her shoulders tightly in front of her. Her features were small, delicate against the soft blackness of her hair. Her skin was pale in the light of the fire and her eyes were in shadow.

Lazair glanced at her and grinned. "A bottle of mescal, honey."

She disappeared and returned in a moment with the bottle in her hand. She approached Lazair reluctantly, handed the bottle to him and turned quickly, but as she did this he reached for her. She felt his hand on her back and dodged out of reach, twisting her body away from him. But his fingers tightened on the scarf and pulled it from her shoulders as she slipped away.

Lew grinned at his chief. "That's a step toward it."

"She likes to play." Lazair felt the material between his fingers and then tore it down the middle.

Lew said, "Maybe she's upset after seeing what you did to her kin."

Lazair folded a part of the scarf lengthwise, then tied it around his neck, sticking the ends into his shirt. "Some girls are funny that way," he said.

Eight

●

"**O** God, by whose mercy the souls of the faithful find rest, vouchsafe to bless this grave, and appoint Thy holy angel to guard it; and release the souls of all those whose bodies are buried here from every bond of sin, that in Thee they may rejoice with Thy saints forever. Through Christ our Lord."

The Franciscan made the sign of the cross in the air and sprinkled the grave with holy water.

Flynn waited patiently, though within him there was an impatience, while the priest finished his prayer over the last grave. He was anxious to be going, but the Franciscan had moved slowly from grave to grave, reciting the burial prayers reverently, a liturgy unaffected by time. There was no need to hurry.

Flynn's restlessness was not out of irreverence. He whispered his prayers with the priest, but his mind kept wandering to the news the vaquero had brought.

As they were lowering the bodies into the freshly dug graves, the vaquero had ridden in, killing his mount with the urgency of his news. He had seen Apaches! Tending his herd, a dozen miles from Soyopa, he had entered a draw after a stray—and there at the other end, trailing down from high country, were the Apaches. He had flown before they were able to see him, he told. But he had looked back once, and coming out of the draw they had traveled southeast in the direction of the deserted village of Valladolid. How many? Perhaps six or seven.

"Then it is not a raiding party," a man had said.

"Who knows the way of the Apache," the vaquero answered. He perspired, and the wide eyes told that he was still frightened.

"What about your cows?"

"My cows must protect themselves."

Flynn had listened with interest. Perhaps this was the opportunity. They could scour the hills for months without finding an Apache. Now, the Apaches had shown themselves. Scout them, he thought. Perhaps they would lead to Soldado Viejo, or, he could even be one of the six. He asked the vaquero to take them back to where he had seen the Apaches, but the vaquero steadfastly refused. Well, they could go alone.

"We might wait a long time for a trail as fresh as this one," he told Bowers.

Bowers shrugged. "Why not? That's why we're here."

A few of the villagers who had heard this looked at the Americans curiously.

They returned to the alcalde's house for their horses, then passed the cemetery again as they left Soyopa by the trail north. Hilario was still standing by the graves. He would move to the foot of a grave, recite the "Hail Mary" and drop a small stone, then move to the next. Later, the villagers would come and do this and after that any traveler entering Soyopa who knew a prayer for the dead would drop a stone.

The vaquero had told them approximately where his small herd had been grazing. Flynn remembered vaguely this country just to the north and the small village of Valladolid, half the size of Soyopa, a lonely outpost for vaqueros and their families. He had passed through it returning home. But now, he was told, Valladolid was only adobe—as lifeless as the mud it was made from. Soldado had struck the vaqueros too often and finally they had left it for larger villages— Soyopa, Rueda and others to the south; though some few herds were still grazed up there in the wild grama and toboso grass.

They rode due north through the afternoon, Flynn a few yards ahead of Bowers. Bowers would make the decisions; it was his assignment. But Flynn would show the way; it was his business.

They found the herd without difficulty, though the cattle were scattered, perhaps thirty head grazing from one end of the meadow to the other. There could be others in the hills now, hidden by the scrub trees, and up the draw which they recognized from the vaquero's description. Flynn did not doubt that the Apaches had driven off some, but until later he was not sure how many.

On the east edge of the meadow they stopped to eat— beef and tortillas which Hilario had told them to take from his house; then followed after the unshod horse tracks as they left the meadow.

At first, Flynn would step down from the saddle often to examine the prints more closely. But in less than a quarter of a mile he was sure and he said to Bowers, "The cowboy wasn't exaggerating. There are six of them. They're driving three cows." Farther on there were horse droppings in the trail. Flynn dismounted again. "They're not expecting anybody to be following."

Bowers said, "How far ahead?"

"About four hours." His eyes swung up to the high country that was before them. "They should be farther than that."

Bowers said, "They're taking their time. Maybe they've forgotten what it's like to be chased."

"What about Lazair?"

Bowers looked at him quickly, curiously, "That rurale mentioned him."

Flynn nodded. "So did Deneen. The rurale thought we

worked for him, and he said something about the hunter of Indians proving to the lieutenant who was boss."

Bowers said, "Hunter of Indians."

"Bounty hunters," Flynn said.

They began climbing shortly after. The ground was high on both sides and the draw rose gradually toward thick scrub brush. Still following the tracks, they crossed a bench then climbed again, now into pine, and soon they reached the long flat crest of the rise. In the distance, the hills took up again, but more rugged—tumbling into each other, spewed with rock and brush, forming a thousand fantastic shapes. The unshod tracks continued on down the slope of the hill, and below them, deathly still in the evening light, was the village of Valladolid.

"Well?" Bowers asked it.

Flynn's eyes roamed over the adobe huts, half squinting. The first buildings were perhaps four hundred yards down the slope. The walls were wind-scarred and the bricks showed in many places where the outer plastering of adobe had crumbled off. Beyond these, a patchwork of brush roof-tops, some caved in or blown away. Grass and brush grew in the streets which they could see, and the taller growth swayed gently as the wind moved through the shadowed lanes. The village seemed all the more dead, because it had once been alive.

Bowers said, "What are you thinking about?"

"All the places down here an Apache could hide," Flynn said.

They moved back into the heavier pines and tied their horses to the lowest branches so they could graze, then sat down to rest and think and check their guns. And for the next hour they smoked cigarettes cupped in their hands and spoke little. When it was almost full dark, Flynn nodded and they rose together and moved back to the slope.

Flynn was starting down the grade as Bowers touched his arm, and he stopped. "Do you really think it's worth it?" Bowers said.

Flynn shrugged. "You have something else you'd rather do?"

"You could lie down there and no one would even know about it."

"The Apaches would. . . ."

Flynn moved off then, Bowers a few yards behind him. They descended slowly, taking their time, and when they had gone almost halfway Flynn motioned to keep lower. The rest of the way they moved more cautiously, zigzagging through the shadows of the brush clumps. Flynn would move ahead, then drop to his stomach and wait for Bowers to follow, then lie motionless to make sure the silence had not changed before moving again. The brush straggled all the way down to the first building, so there was no opening to cross, and when they reached the wall they pressed close to it in the deep shadow of the roof overhang and waited a longer time now.

A cricket chirped inside the house, then another. Flynn eased to the corner of the building, and moved around it holding tight to the wall with his back. He went to a crouch then, passing beneath the small front window. As he disappeared through the doorway the crickets stopped.

Bowers waited at the corner of the house. He counted seconds mechanically, a full minute, while he strained against the silence. Then he followed.

Inside he could see nothing. To the left a window framed the night, shades lighter than the inside darkness, and through it he could make out the dim outline of the next building. He heard Flynn whisper, "Here," and moved toward the sound of his voice.

He touched Flynn before he saw him, against the wall by the window.

"Do you think they're here?"

"Almost dead sure."

"Why?"

Flynn spoke very low, close to Bowers' face. "Because you don't hear anything. Something scared off the night sounds."

The breeze moved through the streets and somewhere a door creaked. It banged—a pistol report against the warped frame—then creaked open again. They were startled by the abruptness of the sound, even though they knew it was the wind.

Flynn said, "Are you afraid?"

Bowers hesitated. "I suppose so."

"Everybody gets scared sometime," Flynn said.

"Do you?"

"Sure."

"Do Apaches?"

"I never asked one. But we might find out." He wanted to see Bowers' face, but it was too dark. "It's not so routine now, is it?"

Bowers said, "No," quietly.

"Do you think you're a better soldier than these Mimbres?"

"I don't know."

"When will you?"

"That's not it."

"It's the not seeing them, isn't it?"

Bowers nodded. "What do you want to do?"

"Take them. If they think we're a bunch they might quit without a fight. Now, they're most likely camped in the square, not chancing getting trapped inside a house. If we can get on two sides and pour it in all of a sudden, we'll catch them with their breechclouts down."

"What if they fight?"

Flynn winked and the tone of his voice meant the same thing. "You'll think of something. That's what they pay you for."

"Go on."

"We're about five houses from the square; you go up this row, I'll cross over a few rows and work around to the other side of the square. Just think of one thing: if it doesn't wear a hat, shoot it."

Bowers saw the form silhouetted in the doorway for a moment, then Flynn was gone.

The cavalryman turned to the window and his body tensed as he lifted his leg and hooked it over the window sill. He paused, sitting on one thigh, before pulling his body through. Then he was out. He moved to the next building and listened for a long minute before going through the window. As he did, the stock of the carbine scraped the inside wall. The sound was rasping, loud in the small room, and Bowers stiffened. He closed his eyes tightly. Finally, when he opened them, he thought: Dammit, hold onto yourself!

Inside, thick darkness again, and the window in the other wall framing the lighter shade of the outside. He went through to the next house, but remained there a longer time while he listened for the sounds that never came, and he tried to picture fear on the face of an Apache.

It took him longer to climb through this window, because now he was more careful. Just keep going, he thought. Don't think and keep going. He dropped to the ground and darted to the next wall keeping his head down. His hand touched the adobe, groped along the crumbling surface; his head came up quickly then and he looked both ways along the wall. But there was no window on this side of the house.

He moved to the corner and inched his face around with his cheek flat to the wall, then sank gradually to hands and knees and crawled along the front of the house, careful of the carbine. At the doorway he paused again, listening, then rose and stepped into the darkness. Instantly the smell touched his nostrils. It hung oppressively in the small room. A raw smell that made him think of blood, and of a butcher's shop.

He started to move and the toe of his foot touched something soft. He stooped then, slowly, extending his hand close to the floor until the palm touched it and told him what it was. Cowhide, and the bloated firmness of the belly. Freshly butchered . . .

Behind him there was a whisper of sound. He knew what it

had to be. Turn and shoot! It flashed in his mind. Don't wait! But it was too late—a hand closed over his mouth . . . something at his throat . . . the carbine jerked from his hand then came back suddenly against his face.

Flynn waited at the rear of the livery stable, his back flat against the boards. He was in shadow, but a few feet from him the sagging door showed plainly in the moonlight. A half-moon, but there were no clouds to obscure its light and the shadows about him hung motionless. Above the doorway a loading tree jutted out dimly against the sky.

The livery stable faced on the square. In the time it had taken to work around to this side, he had heard nothing; and there was no one inside, he was certain of that now; still, they could be just beyond the front entrance. He tried to picture the square as he had once seen it. It was small, with a statue in the middle. The statue of a saint. He calculated now: Anywhere in the square they could not be more than a hundred and fifty feet away. He looked up at the loading tree again, then eased through the partly open doorway and moved along the wall until his hand touched the ladder.

He tested the rungs, the ones he could reach, and as he climbed he pulled carefully on the rungs above him before bringing up his legs. Halfway, the loft was even with his head. He raised the carbine and slid it onto the planking, then raised himself after it. Toward the front, the main loading window showed dimly—a square of night sky, starless, and it grew larger as he crept toward it, easing his weight over the planking. Now and then a squeak, a rusted nail bending—but a small sound that would not carry beyond the building. At the opening he stood to the side and looked straight down over the carbine. There was no sound. No movement.

Flynn moved back now and eased down until he was lying on his stomach. He pushed the Springfield out in front of him, the barrel nosing past the loft edge, and at that moment he saw the Apache.

The Mimbre appeared in a doorway directly across the square, then moved close along the wall until he reached the corner of the building. He crouched then and waited, facing toward the rear of the one-story structure. Flynn raised the Springfield and dropped his head slightly for his cheek to rest against the stock, then swung the barrel less than three inches to bring it against the dim figure of the Mimbre.

He hears something, Flynn thought. That animal sense of his is telling him something. His hand tightened beneath the barrel, feeling the slender balanced weight of the carbine. He wouldn't know what hit him, he thought now. Probably not even hear it. The oil smell of the breech mechanism was strong with his face so close and two inches away his finger crooked over the trigger guard. His thumb raised. Pull it back easy, he thought. He wouldn't hear it, but pull back easy. The thumb closed over the hammer and cocked it.

The figure moved then and the barrel followed him as he glided across the narrow street to the corner of the next house. Flynn saw now that he carried a rifle and was pointing it toward the house behind the one he had just left. It was in the row Bowers would be moving up.

They know he's there, Flynn thought. They must have known it for some time. That's why they aren't in the square. But where are the others? His eyes inched along the adobe fronts across the square. Nothing moved. He swung back to the Apache on the corner. They've filtered back among the buildings and this one is waiting in case he breaks free.

Maybe they've taken him already. And maybe they haven't. But if he breaks for the street, the one on the corner will get him. This went through his mind quickly as he aimed at the Apache, realizing almost at the same time that there was no choice. He must kill the Apache on the chance Bowers wasn't already taken. "Look around," he whispered to the Apache, "then it will be easier." But the figure remained motionless, his back hunched into a round target, as Flynn inhaled slowly, stopped, squeezed the trigger, felt the shock jab against his shoulder, smelled the powder and heard the report echo through the deserted streets. He saw that the Apache had turned as he was hit and was facing him now, lying on his back.

Nine

●

The wind rose, bringing clouds to dim the moonlight, and the wind moved through the streets with a low hissing sound, bending the brush clumps and splattering invisible sand particles against the adobe. The wind moved over the dead Apache, spreading his hair, fanning it into a halo about his head. But this was all, only the wind.

As morning approached, Flynn could see the Apache more plainly. The sun came up behind the stable and a shaft of cold light filtering between the stable and the next building fell directly across the Apache. The shirt would move gently as the breeze stirred, but the curled moccasin toes which pointed to the sky, and the extended arms, palms up, did not move.

Flynn thought: Your friends are probably looking at you at this same moment. One of them saying, "Poor . . ."—something that ends in *i-n* or *y-a* and has a guttural sound to it. Or else something the Mexicans named you. Juan Ladron. Joselito. Or a name like Geronimo which a few years ago was Gokliya. And now they are begging U-sen not to make you walk in eternal darkness, because it wasn't your fault, Flynn continued to think. I'm sorry I killed you at night. It was not the way a warrior should die. But you would have killed me. That's the way it goes. I wish I could light a cigarette.

Where are they, in that house the Mimbre was pointing toward? Probably. With Bowers. Perhaps one has worked his way around and is entering the livery. Flynn rolled to his side and looked back toward the ladder, then to the loft opening again. Just don't start imagining things, he told himself. They'll show sooner or later. It's their move now.

Shortly after he thought this, it came.

His eyes were swinging along the ramada fronts when he caught the movement in the corner of his vision. His eyes slid back instantly to the street where the dead Apache lay. Bowers was standing at the corner of the building. His hands were behind his back.

Flynn watched him, surprised. He had not admitted it, but now he realized that he had supposed Bowers dead.

The cavalryman staggered out from the building suddenly, off balance, and Flynn saw the two Apaches then. One of them pushed Bowers again, staying close behind him, urging him on until they reached the middle of the square and stopped next to the statue. The other Apache followed and now the three of them looked up at the livery stable first, then to the buildings on either side. The Apache behind Bowers jabbed him with his carbine barrel.

Moving his head slowly along the building fronts, Bowers yelled out, "They want me to say something!"

You don't have to say it, Flynn thought. He watched one of the Apaches point the carbine at Bowers' head and pull back the hammer. Give up, or they'll kill him. That doesn't need words. But how do they know I'm still here? And that I'm alone? He thought of their horses then, picketed on the hill. They found the horses. They move fast and they're very thorough, and they know a man wouldn't run off without his horse. Not in this country.

"Flynn . . . don't come out!"

He moved from the opening back to the ladder and

climbed down it wearily. He walked out the wide front door of the stable toward the three figures at the statue. Beyond them, now, he saw two other Apaches standing in the shadow of a wooden awning. The square was dead-still.

The second Apache stepped forward to meet him and he handed the carbine to him, then reached into his coat and drew the pistol and handed this to him.

He said to Bowers, "Well, we tried. What happened?" He saw the bruised cheekbone and the swelling above his right eye.

"I walked into the house where they were butchering a steer," Bowers said. "They were on me before I knew it."

"Red, don't back away from them. Stay calm and we'll get out of this."

Bowers looked at him quickly. It was the first time he had been called that since before the Point. And it had come unexpectedly from Flynn.

The guide looked at the Apache next to him. He said roughly, in Spanish, "What are you called?"

The Apache eyed him narrowly. "Matagente." Then he said in hesitant, word-spaced Spanish, "I do not know you."

"Nor I, you," Flynn said. "But I know you are Mimbreño —and at this time very far from the land of the Warm Springs. But you will come to know us very well. At San Carlos you will see us often."

Matagente's expression did not change as he listened. Now he said, "San Carlos is not for the Warm Springs Apache."

"This is something which ones above us have ordered," Flynn said. "There is no profit in talking about it with you. Where is Soldado? Our words are for him."

"You will see him," Matagente said. He motioned with the carbine, saying no more, directing them toward the house where the others stood. They had carried the dead Apache from the street and now he was under the ramada near the doorway. Matagente looked at him as he prodded the two men into the house, but still he said nothing.

*   *   *

They sat on the packed-dirt floor with their legs crossed and their backs to the wall and waited. For what, they did not know, wondering why they were not taken to the Apaches' ranchería.

Matagente brought them meat, then sat near the doorway with one of the Springfields across his lap. His hand moved over the smooth stock idly. Before this he had used a Burnside .54 which needed percussion caps and powder, and often it misfired.

When they had eaten the meat, Flynn said, "Take us to Soldado now."

"You will see him," Matagente said, and again lapsed into silence. This new gun was in his mind—this pesh-e-gar—and he was thinking how good it would be to fire it.

Through the doorway Flynn could see the other Apaches standing in front of the house, talking to each other in low tones he could not hear. Then he saw them look up. One of them moved off and the others watched after him. In a moment he was back and he called in to Matagente, in the Mimbreño dialect. "They are here."

Matagente rose and moved to the doorway as mounted Apaches suddenly appeared in front of the house. These dismounted as others continued to enter the square from the side street, walking their ponies. The sound of this came to Flynn, but he could see nothing until Matagente stepped back from the doorway. He saw the Apaches now, at least twenty, probably more, milling in front of the house, then his view was blocked again as a figure moved into the doorway.

Matagente said, "Now you see Soldado. Tell him your story, American."

Bowers looked at him with open surprise, and now wondered why he had expected this Apache to look different than any other, though he was old for an Apache still active. Wrinkled face and eyes half closed beneath the bright red headband. And skinny—filthy clothes, ill-fitting to make him seem smaller. A buttonless cavalry jacket, a bandoleer crossing his chest holding the jacket only partly closed, and cotton trousers stuffed into curl-toed moccasins that reached to his knees where they folded and tied. He rested one hand on the butt of a cap-and-ball dragoon pistol in his waistband. But the hand only rested there; it was not a threat.

Flynn watched his face as he sat down in front of them crossing his legs. The cavalry guide had expected nothing. A man is some things and he is not others. A Mimbre Apache is not a fashion plate. He is ragged and dirty and has the odor of an unwashed dog and at night in his ranchería drinks tizwin until it puts him to sleep or sends him after a woman. He has many faults—by white standards. But he is a guerrilla fighter, and in his own element he is unbeatable. That's the thing to remember, Flynn thought. Don't underestimate him because he smells. He isn't chief because his dad was. And a broncho chief doesn't get to be as old as he is on his good looks.

He said now, in Spanish, "Do you speak English?"

The Apache shook his head.

"Lieutenant, you can take that for what it's worth. He might speak it better than we do." Then to Soldado he said, "We did not come here to fight your men. The fight could not be avoided."

"But one of them is dead," Soldado said.

"I did not wish him to die the way he did, but it could not be helped. It is not the way a Mimbreño should die."

The old chief looked at him intently. "Who of us have you known?"

"I have known Victorio and Chee and Old Nana."

"What are you called?"

"Davíd Flín." He pronounced the name slowly.

"I have not heard of you."

"This country is wide."

The Apache said quietly, "Yet you would force us to live in one small corner of it."

"What I do," Flynn said, "is not entirely of my mind."

"Then perhaps you are a fool."

"It is only foolish when you fight against what is bound to happen," Flynn said. "I see the days of the Mimbreño numbered . . . as well as the Chiricahua, Coyotero, Jicarilla and the Mescalero. The Tonto and Mojave have already been given their own land."

"And who is this that gives land which he does not own?" the Apache asked.

Damn him, Flynn thought. He said, "The chief of the Americans, who owns it because of his power. Let me tell you something, old man, for your wisdom to absorb: your days remaining are few. If you give yourself up now, you will be given good land which still abounds in those things to keep you alive. And you will be under the protection of our government."

Soldado said seriously, "And if I were to find my woman lying with someone else and I cut off her nose, what would happen to me?"

"You would be taken before the agent," Flynn said, feeling foolish saying the words.

"For what reason?"

"For your offense."

"And when our women see that they can lie with any man they wish and only the husband is punished if he objects, what will your government do then?"

"Your women are your own problem," Flynn said.

"Man, we have many problems which we would keep our own."

Flynn shook his head wearily. What a sly old bastard, he thought. He makes you sound like a damn fool. Maybe you can't be a big brother. Maybe the only kind of respect they know is a kick in the face. He intimated so just now with that about the women. Only you're not in a very good spot to do any kicking. All you can do now is bluff—and if it doesn't work, which it probably won't, you haven't lost anything.

He said now to Soldado, "I tell you this as a friend: If you fight, you will be defeated, and being remembered with distaste you will be treated ill and perhaps be put into prison."

Soldado said, "What is the difference in meaning between these words prison and reservation?"

"You ask many questions."

"I only wish to borrow from the wisdom of the American," Soldado said.

"You may scoff at these words," Flynn said, "but what happens, happens. It is above you and me and will come about regardless of what you do, but I am wise enough to see it."

"Are you wise enough to see your own fate, American?"

"I speak to you as a people."

"And I speak to you as a man. What does this spirit of yours say will happen to you?"

"I could die at this moment," Flynn said. "So could you."

"But who would you say this is more likely to happen to?"

You're not doing this very good, Flynn thought to himself. He always has the last word and makes you feel like a green kid who doesn't know what he's doing. Bowers touched his arm then and as he looked at him Bowers said, "How does he know why we're here?"

"What?"

"You've told him nothing. We could be scalp hunters for all he knows, yet he talks about the reservation. How does he know we came to see him?"

Soldado said, "The silent one wonders how I know of your mission."

In English, Flynn said quickly, "How did you know what he said?"

Soldado shook his head. *"No comprendo."*

Flynn repeated the question in Spanish and the old Indian smiled faintly. "His question was on his face. It did not need words; though I have been waiting for you to ask it."

"Then you have known of us for some time," Bowers said.

"Since the day you gathered the bodies of the *Nakai-yes* and returned them to their village. This was not an act of the killers of Indians."

Flynn concealed his amazement. Now he said, "You were very thorough. No one was left alive."

Soldado studied him silently before saying, "Do you believe these words you use?" and when Flynn did not answer, he said, "No, you do not believe them, but you would hear it aloud that we did not kill the *Nakai-yes*. There is no need however to explain these things to the wise American who is able to see the future."

But it was the past Flynn was seeing as the old Indian spoke. Burned wagon and the lifeless bodies in a narrow draw, and he tried to picture white men having done this. Before, he had been almost certain that this was not the work of Apaches. Still, he could not bring himself to believe that it had been white men. "How do you know who did this?" he said now.

Soldado smiled faintly. "Once, at night, I sat before my jacale and in front of me there was a mound of stones. There were red stones and white stones, which I could see by the light of the fire. And I played this game with myself, taking all of the red stones and placing them here," he said, gesturing with his hands, "and soon, all of the stones remaining before me were white." His smile broadened. "That is how I look into the past, American."

"These men will be punished for their deeds," Flynn said.

"By your government?"

"Yes, by my government. By men who act in its behalf."

"And who are these men?"

"I speak of this one whom I serve," Flynn said, nodding to Bowers, "and myself."

Soldado said, "Yet the one who serves is the spokesman."

"I speak when the ones before us are not worthy of his voice."

"But only worthy of his wonder," the Apache said confidently.

"You will be the one to wonder, soon, when you are a witness to his power."

"And what if you are already dead?"

"Your threat is nothing against the power of this man who is silent. And remember these words well, old man. As the hunters of Indians are destroyed, so will you be. They have already aroused his vengeance, which is what you are doing now. For I swear by the sacred pollen which you carry to ward off evil, that if you do not follow us in peace, you will be dragged to San Carlos behind our horses."

The Apache's face was expressionless. The eyes half closed, sleepily. He stared at Flynn a long moment, then his gaze swung to Bowers and as it did he drew the dragoon pistol from his waistband. He raised it slowly, cocking it, then straightened his arm, aiming the long barrel at Bowers and said, "Where is his power now, American?"

Flynn said nothing.

The Apache lowered the gun, looking toward Flynn again. He said, "Do you speak in the tongue of the Mimbreño?"

Flynn was surprised, but he nodded. "I speak some."

"Good. Then you will come to the ranchería." To Matagente, he said, "You will conduct them with three men. The rest of us will come at night tomorrow when this raid is terminated." He said to Flynn, as explanation, "We have only stopped here for meat."

Flynn was puzzled. He said, "And why is it necessary that I speak Mimbre?"

Soldado smiled, showing yellowed teeth. "So that you may tell our children your story."

Ten

•

"**I**'m leaving now," Rellis said.

Lazair was looking toward the tarp shelter of the cave, following the girl's movements as she gathered the tin plates, scraping and stacking them, and as she picked them up she glanced toward Lazair then turned away quickly when she saw that he was watching her. The two men were standing by the cook fire; Rellis, with his bay mare behind him.

"I said I'm leaving," Rellis repeated, impatiently.

"Well, go on." Lazair still watched the cave, though the girl had gone in now.

"I'm taking some men with me."

Lazair looked at him now. "Are you asking me or telling me?"

"Take it any way you want."

Lazair smiled faintly. "You're pretty tough, aren't you?"

"I get by."

"You'll get by with four men today," Lazair said quietly. "Lew and Warren are going back. Tell Lew to bring two more." He waited, but Rellis made no reply.

"Doesn't that suit you?"

Rellis shrugged lazily, but his eyes were hard on the other man's face. "They tell me you're the boss."

"You don't sound like you're sure of it."

He shrugged again. "You can't believe everything you hear."

There was a silence. Then Lazair said quietly, "Believe it, Frank. Even if you never believe anything else." He turned away then and moved off toward the cave, taking his time.

Rellis mounted the bay, then looked after Lazair a long moment before calling to the men standing off by the horses. They stared up at him idly.

"Lew, you and Warren . . . and two more!"

Lew Embree nodded to two of the men and one of them said, "We got us another boss." Rellis was moving off and did not hear him. They mounted then, resignedly, and followed Rellis down through the defile to the meadow.

Lew glanced up to the rocks and shouted, "Wesley, you keep awake, now!" to the guard, and then laughed. Warren laughed with him. They crossed the meadow at a trot, but slowed to a walk as the grass sloped over into the pines, beginning the long winding descent. Down farther, where the trail widened, Lew spurred to ride next to Rellis.

"Curt's going to get that girl yet, you wait and see." Lew grinned.

"I don't give a damn who he gets," Rellis answered shortly. Then he said, "How far to the pueblo?"

"About three, four hours," Lew said. "Depending how fast you go."

"I want to get there quick."

"The country ain't built for going too fast. She closes in on you and you can't see ahead in some places."

"I'm not looking for anything."

"But the 'Paches might be looking for you."

Rellis turned on one hip to look at Lew. "You scared of them?"

"Much as anybody else is," Lew said. "It's when you can't see 'em but can feel 'em is when I'm scared. Like just seeing their smoke curling up in the hills and then when you get on ahead there's another smoke rise and you know they're passing the word that you're coming. We was over deeper in the Madres once and we seen this smoke, but we kept going and soon there was this canyon that was still as a tomb—just rocks that went up and up and up and then sky. There wasn't a sound but the horses. Then if you'd listen close, you'd hear the wind playing over the rocks. You'd stretch your neck looking up those walls and there was just that dead stillness . . . and the hum of the breeze, which you didn't count because it would be there even if nobody was about.

"We moved down the middle, about fifty yards from both sides. Then all of a sudden I heard this swish and a thud and right next to me Wesley's brother . . . you know that boy that was on guard? . . . Wes's brother falls out of the saddle with a arrow sticking out of his neck. Mister, we got out of there fast."

"Was Curt there?" Rellis said.

"Sure he was there."

"You feel any 'Paches now?"

"I feel 'em most every time I ride to the pueblo."

"Maybe you should've stayed back there with Curt."

"Maybe I'd like to have."

Rellis said now, "He doesn't care much what happens to you or the rest, does he?"

"What do you mean?"

"He would've sent you and Warren back alone if I hadn't been going out and said something."

"We rode in alone."

"That's what I mean," Rellis said. "He knows there's 'Paches around. How come you and Warren got to ride back and forth alone?"

"You can get used to anything," Lew said, looking at Rellis closely now, "even a feeling."

"Just sits there working up his nerve to grab chiquita and lets you do all the work."

"You don't like it?"

"Hell no."

"Why don't you get out then?"

Rellis looked at him. "Just keep your goddamn nose where it belongs."

"You do a lot of pushing for one man."

"You going to do anything about it?"

Lew said nothing.

"Then keep your mouth shut."

"A man's got to talk about something."

Rellis did not answer. He rolled a cigarette and drew on it without taking it from his mouth, watching the trail.

For a short while, Lew remained silent, then he said, "I'm going up ahead a ways and look around." Rellis shrugged and Lew said, half turning in the saddle, "Warren, come on."

Rellis watched them move off, bearing to the right, climbing to higher ground, parallel with the trail but into the pines where they could watch the country below without being seen.

He pinched the cigarette stub from his mouth and ground it out between his fingers, crumbling tobacco and paper, then let the breeze take the particles from his open palm. His eyes, light colored, mild, and contrasting oddly with the coarseness of his features, were focused on the trail ahead, because you had to be careful. And partly because he was thinking and did not want distractions. Thinking about what he would do to a tall, thin man with a light mustache who wore a shoulder rig and who thought he was so goddamn smart. You should have pulled the trigger. What the hell was wrong with you! he thought. Well, you won't back down next time. Then he thought: I didn't back down! The son of a bitch had something under the cloth. He wouldn't have been so smart if he hadn't. You played it careful, that's all. He won't have a chance to get anything ready this time. And it's him, all right. It's his description. And I can even feel it's him, the son of a bitch.

He thought of the things he could do to Flynn. Get him when he's turned around and go up behind him and say something like . . . "Aren't you going to say hello to your old friend?" And when the son of a bitch turns around, jam the pistol into his gut and let go . . . and watch the expression on his face . . . He smiled thinking of this. And if that other one's with him, he'll get his, too. Like that old man with the beard who thought he was so smart laughing all the time.

Then Warren was standing just off the trail in a small clearing. His horse was not in sight. He held one hand palm-toward-them and the other hand was to his mouth.

Rellis dismounted and led his horse toward him. "What's the matter?"

" 'Paches."

"Where?"

"Down below. Going into a draw that comes out just up a ways from where Lew is now."

"How many?"

"Six. But two of them have got hats on."

They left their horses and followed Warren up through the pines, then, just ahead, they could see Lew belly-down behind the rocks, his carbine pointing down the draw. Farther back, the trough between the hills was dense with trees, but here the trees thinned as the draw climbed into a rise, its steep sides falling gradually away. Lew's carbine pointed to where the riders would come out of the trees. He glanced around as he heard the others come up.

"Don't make a sound."

Rellis eased down next to him and the other spread out along the rocks.

"We ought to have somebody over on the other side," Lew said, "But it's too late now."

"Where are they?" Rellis said.

"They'll show any minute." Lew pointed with the carbine barrel. "Come out right over there and pass within a hundred feet."

Rellis said, "Five against six," considering this.

"They won't have a chance."

"What's this about two of them wearing hats?"

"They was way off when I spotted them but that's what it looked like."

"I never heard of that."

Lew said, "I seen reservation 'Paches wearing hats." He raised himself on his elbows and looked toward the others down the line then to Rellis, "If we do this right," he said, "we got us six hundred pesos in the bank."

Rellis said nothing. He had both a carbine and a shotgun with him, and now he was examining the shotgun. At this range the shotgun would be better, especially if they rode close together.

Suddenly he heard Lew whisper, "Here they come. Get ready."

A lone Apache came out of the trees slowly, cautiously. He rode directly up the middle of the draw, holding his pony to a walk. Near the rise, he angled toward the far side and as he reached the slope, two more appeared from the trees coming out into the open. They scanned both sides of the draw as they drew closer to the rise. One of them rode straight ahead, urging his pony up the rise. The other followed for a short distance, then veered abruptly, coming toward the near side. He stopped suddenly and his eyes crawled over the rimrock.

Rellis whispered to Lew, "Take him. I'll get the one on the rise." His head turned to Warren. "The one on the other side. Tell the others."

"That's only three of them," Lew whispered hoarsely.

"We can't wait forever . . . take him!"

Lew squinted down the short barrel as Rellis swung the shotgun toward the Apache who had stopped at the crest of the rise.

Flynn felt his horse's head jerk suddenly and saw that the Apache was leading them off to the side toward the hill slope. A line trailed from the Apache's horse, back through the bit ring of Flynn's bridle to Bowers' and was tied there.

Their hands were lashed to the saddle horns. Ahead, they could see Matagente and the two other Apaches disappearing into the trees.

Bowers said, "Did you make out what he told them?"

"He said they'd go on up to that rise . . . see it way up there over the trees? . . . and signal for us to follow."

"Doesn't take any chances."

"They never do," Flynn said.

The Apache, with one of their Springfields across his lap, was looking intently toward the rise. He glanced toward them then and muttered gutturally.

Bowers said, "What was that?"

"Mimbre for shut-up," Flynn said.

They kept their eyes on the rise. It was perhaps a quarter of a mile above them, but seemed much closer because of the height. Then one of the Apaches was visible past the dense tops of the trees, a small speck moving gradually up the slope. They watched him reach the crest and stop there, and he seemed to wait there uncertainly before turning his mount to face back down the draw.

He sat erect on the pony's back and raised his hand to shield the glare from his eyes, looking over the trees below him. Then the other hand raised a carbine high overhead and waved it once in a long sweeping motion. And as if on the signal, gunfire cut the stillness, echoing down the draw.

The Apache clung low to the pony and started to move off, but he was sliding to the side and as the horse broke he fell, grabbing wildly for the mane, and rolled down out of sight. There were more shots, but from below they could see no one.

The Mimbre did not hesitate. Flynn swore. Bowers yelled as he cut past them suddenly. The lead rope turned their horses abruptly, jerked from standstill to dead-run as he swerved out into the draw and back down the way they had come. They dodged after the Mimbre through the scattering of trees and brush scraping mesquite thickets, riding head-down, unable to raise their arms against the branches. The lead rope would slacken, then tighten suddenly to stagger their mounts off balance, though neither of them went down. When they reached open country the Mimbre paused to listen, but now there was no sound of firing. And he moved off again at a sharp right angle, skirting the base of the hills. Soon, though, he angled into the hills again, now leading them much slower.

"You never know, do you?" Bowers said.

"Not in this country."

"It's either rurales or this Lazair," Bowers considered, and when the scout nodded, he said, "Where's he going now?"

"He'll want to take a look before running for home."

"With us along?"

"Maybe he's got plans for us," Flynn said.

They moved up into high country behind the Apache who would stop frequently to listen; climbing slowly because there was no trail, winding into natural switchbacks where the ground rose steeper, transforming itself into jagged rock formations. But always there were dense pines scattered, straggling over the slopes, and they kept to the dimness of the trees most of the time. The sunlight clung to the open areas, coldly reflecting on the grotesque stone shapes—shadowed crevices and the brush clumps that stirred lazily when the wind would rise.

And over it all, a stillness.

For a time, as they climbed, the cry of a verdin followed them. But when they looked up into the trees the bird was never there—hidden against the flat shade of a tree limb. A thin, bodiless cry in the stillness. Just before they stopped they saw the verdin suddenly rise from a cholla bush and disappear into the glare, and they did not hear him again.

The Mimbre led them into a hollow that was steep on three sides with shelf rock, ending abruptly only a dozen yards beyond the brush fringe of the entrance. He dismounted, dropping the Springfield, and approached Flynn's horse.

He looked up at the scout steadily for a moment then

moved in close and quickly unstrapped the latigo. He grabbed Flynn's leg suddenly and pulled, dragging him down with his saddle. He moved to Bowers then and did the same thing, and now both of them were on the ground still astride their saddles. If they were to move, they would have to drag the saddles between their legs. The Mimbre picked up the Springfield, then glanced at them once more before disappearing through the brush.

Rest easy, Flynn thought. He saw Bowers begin to strain at the rawhide that was squeezing his wrists and he said quickly, "Not yet!" Bowers looked up and he added quietly, "He's watching us. Give him time to calm down and get out."

"How do you know?"

"Wouldn't you?" Flynn said.

Bowers relaxed, squatting hunched over the saddle, and his fingers moved idly against the saddle horn. It would be easy to drag the saddle over and untie Flynn's hands, since his fingers were free, and he could not understand this. Finally he said, "We can get out of this. Why didn't he tie us to a tree?"

"Because he'd have to free our hands to do it," Flynn said. "He didn't want to take a chance, and this is the next best thing. He's more concerned with those others over in the draw—close friends, maybe a brother."

"Why didn't he kill us?"

"I don't know. Maybe for the same reason Soldado did not."

Bowers frowned. "Which was what?"

"You'd have to ask an Apache," Flynn said.

Bowers said nothing now, listening to the silence, staring up at the shelf rock and the sky directly above them and over the brush fringe at the entrance. The hollow was in deep shadow because now the sun was off to the west. After a time he shook his head wearily.

"It's a god-awful poor way to fight a war," he said.

Flynn looked at him. "What war?"

"Whatever you want to call it then," Bowers said irritably.

"No cannons."

"You can keep the cannon."

"It's a good thing that old Apache doesn't have any."

"Or the rurales . . . or this Lazair," Bowers said. "I'm trying to make up my mind who's the worst of the three."

Flynn said quietly, "I don't think there's any doubt."

Bowers thought of the wagon train now, and of the girl and what the old Apache had said about the red stones and the white stones and he knew what Flynn meant. And he said nothing. But after a while, after he had thought of Flynn and the girl and Flynn's never mentioning the girl, he became angry and he thought: He's been fighting Apaches so long he acts like one. No emotions. Just a stoicism—like a rock.

They waited for almost two hours, talking in low tones when they did talk, and now there was little light showing over the brush fringe. Then, "It's about that time," Flynn said matter-of-factly. "Let's get out of here."

Bowers looked at him as the cavalry guide rose and dragged over his saddle and pushed it tight against Bowers. His fingers strained away from the rawhide until he touched Bowers' hand, then the fingers worked at the rawhide slowly because the knots were stiff and he did not have the full strength of his hands to use. But finally the thong loosened and Bowers was free. He untied the guide's hands. They passed through the brush cover and moved off in a general southwest direction toward Soyopa.

But when it was full dark, they stopped. A niche in the rocks would protect them from the wind. There was no fire; and before lying down, Flynn placed a semicircle of loose stones out a few yards from the niche. Then they slept; even with the chill and the wind moaning over the rocks. The Apaches had prevented sleep entirely the night before. And the dead had made it fitful the night before that.

They moved off again with the first light, past the circle of stones that were still in place.

"We're above that draw now," Flynn said. "The Mimbre

brought us almost clear around it to the other side." He pointed far off over the trees to the wild country that fell below them. "It's down in there somewhere. If we head about that way we'll cross it . . . maybe find out what happened."

As they moved on, working their way down, Bowers said suddenly, "You've got the biggest capacity for doing things of any man I know."

"It's a big country. Everything in it's big," Flynn said. "The sun's big, the mountains, the deserts, even the bugs. You got to strain to keep up with it, that's all."

"What are you going to get out of this?" Bowers said.

"Sore feet."

"You know what I mean."

"Four dollars a day."

"What else?"

"What do you want, Red, a medal for everything you do?"

"I want a good reason, that's all!"

"Isn't that colonel reason enough?"

"You haven't answered my question."

Flynn's eyes lifted from Bowers and moved along the wall of rocky slope that rimmed this end of the clearing they had entered minutes before. He glanced off in the other direction, at the flat meadow that offered no cover, then back to the rocks and he saw it again—remaining fixed now, a sliver of light pointing out from a crevice in the rocks—like sun reflecting on a gun barrel.

"Mister, you'll have to ask me some other time," he said. "I think we're walking into something."

Eleven

●

"**H**old it there!"

It came abruptly then to stop them fifty feet from the sloping rock wall. Bowers' eyes went over the slope and Flynn said, "About ten o'clock, just above those two boulders." He saw it now, the gun barrel hanging motionless, pointing down through the crevice. No one showed behind it.

"Throw your guns away!"

Flynn's eyes stayed on the crevice. "We're unarmed!"

"I'll give you five seconds."

"We don't have any!"

A silence followed. Then, "Take off your coats and walk slow with your hands in the air."

They did this and as they reached the slope, the man appeared. He descended part way until he was only a few yards above them. He stopped here, squatting on a shelf, with a double-barreled shotgun pointing down toward them.

"What do you want?"

"We're on our way to Soyopa," Flynn said.

"Just out for a little stroll?"

"You're close."

The man grinned, raising the shotgun. "You better say something that makes sense."

Bowers said impatiently, "We need horses, does that make sense?"

The man nodded, taking his time, "But I want to know what you're doing here."

Flynn said, "Get off that rock and take us to Lazair and quit wasting everybody's time." The man looked at him startled and he knew he had guessed it right.

"How do you know he's here?"

"You going to take us, or d'you want me to start yelling for him?"

The man studied them silently, then shrugged, as if he had carried it as far as he could. He said, "Move on into that pass yonder and follow it up." And as they entered the defile he came down and stayed a few feet behind them until the pass opened up into the pocket high in the rocks.

The camp seemed deserted—no one about the four tents, the cook fire dead and over by the cave the only movement was the tarp awning moving gently with the breeze. The guard mumbled, "Where the hell is everybody . . ." Then he saw them, seven or eight men off beyond the tents, standing idly before a patch of young aspen. "They're over there," he said, and motioned them to go on.

The men looked toward them as they approached. One of them had his back turned, squatting at the base of an aspen and he looked over his shoulder but did not get up. The man with the shotgun yelled, "Somebody fetch Curt!"

For a moment no one moved and someone said, "What's the matter with you?" Then one of them walked off toward the tarp shelter. The others stood where they were, staring at the newcomers, and the one who had been squatting rose now to study them also. Something was behind him, huddled at the base of the aspen—a shoulder, and an arm bent back to the tree trunk.

The guard said, "You still at it?"

"What does it look like?"

Another one said, "The son of a bitch won't even groan."

He stepped aside to reveal the half-naked figure of a man,

a dark man with hair to his shoulders, a breechclout and curl-toed moccasins. His upper body sagged limply from the white bark, head-down, hands bound behind the trunk. And he sat heavily with his legs extended, the left thigh bloody, dried blood and a gaping raw wound. His upper body and head showed bruises and in many places the blood ran down his body.

Flynn leaned closer to him, and as if the Indian could feel his presence he looked up slowly. It was Matagente, his face beaten almost beyond recognition.

Flynn said gently, in Mimbreño, "What do they do to you?" But the head went down and the Apache did not answer.

He heard someone say, "Who are they?" and he looked up to see the guard shrug his shoulders; then, past him, he saw a man standing in the cave entrance, holding the blanket covering aside, watching them. Flynn rose and now saw the blanket hanging smooth again and the man was not there. But in a moment he reappeared and now came from the shelter toward them.

Lazair said nothing, studying them, then glanced toward the guard. "Who's on watch?"

"I am."

"You ain't going to see a hell of a lot from here." He waited until the guard moved off before returning his gaze to Bowers and Flynn. "Well?" he said.

Flynn nodded to Matagente. "What happened to the others?"

"Dead," Lazair said. He eyed them coldly, his face shadowed beneath a willow-root straw. The brim curled, pointed low over his thin nose. He stood in a half-slouch, his shirt open almost to the waist, but the bright red kerchief tight about his throat. He said, "How'd you know there were any more?"

"That one had us when you hit him," Flynn said.

"Small goddamn world. My boys brought him in yesterday."

"What are you doing to him?"

"Why?"

"Just curious."

"Asking him where the old chief lives."

"You don't expect him to tell you?"

Lazair shrugged. "No skin off my tail. It's up to him. He tells or he wakes up dead."

"I hear the old man's got five hundred pesos on his head," Flynn said.

"You heard wrong. It's eight hundred now." Lazair nodded toward Matagente. "His lieutenant's got three hundred." He smiled faintly. "The price of fame, eh?"

Flynn said quietly, "How much is your hair worth?"

Lazair studied him. "You can talk plainer than that."

"I've seen your picture somewhere . . . on a dodger."

"Where would that be?"

"Cibucu, Fort Thomas, somewhere like that."

Lazair grinned. "You're Army, eh? Goddamn Lew was right . . . for once in his life. You're a little out of your territory."

Bowers said now, "So are a few Mimbreño Apaches."

Lazair looked him up and down, noticing the issue belt and holster and the high boots. "Where's your uniform?" he said. He smiled again pushing back the straw from his forehead. "They sent the two of you all the way down here after Apaches?" He shook his head, still grinning. "That's the goddamnedest thing I ever heard. What do you expect to do?"

Flynn said, "Talk that old Mimbre into being a farmer."

Lazair shifted his eyes to him. "You think he'll mind?"

"He might."

Lazair shook his head again, because he still couldn't believe it. "You mean to tell me they sent just two of you?"

Bowers said, "That's right."

"Christ, I've got fourteen men and we've never laid eyes on him!"

"He's seen you, though," Bowers said. "He was talking about it yesterday."

"Where?"

"Not far from here," Bowers said.

"If your men weren't so gun-happy," Flynn said, "they could have followed that one," he nodded toward Matagente, "right to the ranchería." He looked at the men standing off from him. "He had my guns with him—a Springfield swing-block and an altered .44, the ramrod and lever off, with an ejector on the right side of the barrel."

Lazair's men returned his stare silently, hostilely.

He looked at Lazair. "D. F. was carved on the stock of the Springfield. Do I look for them, or do you tell somebody to hand them over?"

Lazair picked a cigar from his shirt pocket and as he lighted the end his eyes remained on Flynn. He exhaled the smoke leisurely. "Maybe we'd better wait," he said.

"Long as I get them."

"Where'd the old man say he was going?"

"He didn't."

"But he was going to come home and tend to you later, eh?"

Flynn nodded.

"Maybe," Lazair said grinning, "I ought to just follow you around if I want to find old Soldado."

Bowers looked surprised. "You're not holding us?"

"Why?"

"We might be cutting into your business."

"Do I look worried to you? Hell, you can go any place you like . . . even give you a couple of mounts to use. Anything to help the Army." He smiled sardonically, his teeth clenched on the cigar. "Goddamnedest thing I ever heard of. You're down here hunting him against the law 'cause you're on the wrong side of the fence, and I do the same thing and get paid for it 'cause I'm in a legitimate business."

"We'll have to have a drink over that sometime," Flynn said.

"Next time I'm in Soyopa."

Flynn glanced toward the cave. "Don't you have anything?"

"Not today," Lazair said. "You going back now?"

Flynn nodded.

"There's a friend of yours in town," Lazair said. "Matter of fact he was the one ambushed those Indians yesterday. Brought in this one 'cause he was still alive, then rode out this morning for Soyopa. One of the boys saw you in town and this one thinks he might know you." He watched Flynn slyly. "Name of Rellis. That ring any bells?"

Flynn hesitated and his face showed a natural surprise. "Frank Rellis . . . I'd like to see him again."

Lazair prompted, "He didn't say where he knew you."

"In Contention."

"Nice place . . . I've been there." Lazair glanced at his men. "Who's got this man's guns?"

No one spoke.

His eyes went over them. "Sid?"

The man said nothing.

"Goddamn it I'm talking to you!"

The one called Sid, heavy-set, with a stubble of red beard, stepped out reluctantly and drew Flynn's pistol from his belt. "The carbine's in the tent," he mumbled.

"Here, let's see it," Lazair said. He weighted the pistol in his hand. "Just a mite long in the barrel. Likely it's accurate, though." His arm swung quickly thumbing the hammer and he fired the pistol in the motion.

Sid jumped quickly. "Hey!"

But no one was looking at him. Matagente sagged forward, his chin against his chest, unmoving, and below his chin was the small hole Lazair's bullet had made.

"Damn accurate," Lazair said.

A silence followed. Flynn studied him coldly. "You trying to prove something?"

Lazair shrugged. "He wasn't doing anybody much good. Hair's worth more'n his carcass. See, we don't exactly make farmers out of them, but we help the crops . . . turn them under, like manure."

He handed the pistol to Flynn. "You ought to cut that barrel down. Sid," he said over his shoulder, "you saddle up two mounts and fetch that carbine along and if anybody's got this other soldier's gun, fork over." He nodded to Bowers and Flynn. "You boys take it easy now." He turned and walked off toward the cave.

It was past noon when they reached Soyopa, entering by the way they had gone out two days before. And now the cemetery was silent. Rows of wooden crosses, but no one kneeling to remember the dead. Later on, when the shadows lengthened behind the church, the women would come. Always someone came.

The newer graves were near the road and already these were beginning to resemble the others, though the wooden crosses were not yet graved by the weather; small stones spread over the low mounds—a stone for a prayer for the repose of the soul.

Flynn dismounted stiffly and walked to the grave of Anastacio Esteban. Bowers followed him. A square of wood was nailed to the arms of the cross and it bore the inscription:

> *Aquí yace Anastacio María Esteban*
> *Vencino de Soyopa*
> *Matado por los barbaros*
> *el dia 26 de Octubre del año 1876*
> *Ora por el, Christiano, por Dios.*

Flynn said in English, "Killed by the barbarians. . . . Christian, for the sake of God, pray for his soul." Then he said again, *"Matado por los barbaros. . . ."* He looked at Bowers. "A barbarian with a willow-root straw and a red neckerchief."

Bowers eyed him curiously. "You're sure?"

"Absolutely."

"The Indian could have been lying."

"It's not what Soldado said."

Bowers looked at him, but said nothing.

"Then you didn't see her," Flynn said, ". . . just for a moment in the cave entrance. Nita Esteban."

Twelve

●

A breeze moved over the square, raising dust swirls about the stone obelisk.

Two rurales lounged asleep in the shade of Duro's headquarters, and in front of Las Quince Letras a row of horses stood at the tie rack—a dun swished its tail lazily and the flanks of a big chestnut quivered to shake off flies. A dog yelped somewhere beyond the adobe fronts. And a woman, a black mantilla covering her head and shoulders, passed without sound into the shadowed doorway of Santo Tomás de Aquín. In the heat of the afternoon it was best to remain within.

From the doorway that opened onto the balcony, Lamas Duro watched the man leave the mescal shop and cross the square to the adobe whose sign read Comida. He walked leisurely, carrying a bottle of something.

"One of the American filth," Duro said half aloud.

As the figure passed from view he saw two riders then enter the square from the street that bordered the church, and as they passed the mescal shop Duro moved back into the room, buttoning his shirt. He smoothed his hair with his fingers as his eyes went on the desk to see the mescal bottle and glass. Hastily now he gathered them up, finishing the inch of colorless sweet liquid in the glass, and disappeared into the bedroom. He was back in a moment and arranged the papers on his desk in a semblance of order before returning to the doorway. The two riders were almost directly below.

He stepped out onto the balcony and called down, "Señores, please come up!" his smile as white as his shirt.

The taste of mescal was sour in his mouth and he lighted a cigar as he listened to the double tread on the stairs. Then they were on the balcony and he stepped aside allowing them to enter the room first.

"You do me an honor, Señor Flín and Lieutenant Bowers."

Bowers looked at him quickly.

Duro smiled. "This is a small pueblo, Lieutenant. The news does not have far to travel. Perhaps the alcalde tells a close friend . . . or someone overheard you speaking. He tells a friend. It enters Las Quince Letras and *pop* . . . it is out."

"Our identity was not intended to be kept secret," Bowers said.

"Of course not." Duro smiled. "But I wouldn't blame you if you did intend it so. Sometimes there is a problem in crossing into another country to perform a mission of a government nature. Often such matters must be handled with discretion. Of course, here you have nothing to fear. As a representative of Porfirio Diaz, I am at your command."

"That's very kind of you," Bowers said woodenly.

"Not at all." Duro held up his hand as if he would not think of accepting gratitude. "I know His Excellency, Porfirio, would have instructed that I aid your mission in every way . . . had he been informed of it. After all, the menace of the Apaches is a reason for the existence of our rurales. Actually then, you are giving assistance to us. Though I cannot say I envy your task." He said this as one soldier to another.

Bowers said, "But as a military man you know one cannot question his orders."

"Certainly." Duro bowed.

Flynn's eyes went over the room and returned to the rurale. "Have you ever made contact with Soldado Viejo?"

Duro shook his head. "Not with that elusive one. A few times, though, we have taken others of his tribe. The day you arrived we executed one." He sighed. "Sometimes such an act seems without heart but," his eyes shifted to Bowers, "one cannot question his orders."

Flynn crooked a knuckle to stroke his mustache idly. "I suppose not," he said. "You don't have to pay out much bounty money then."

"Occasionally." Duro shrugged.

"We were talking to a man named Lazair this morning—"

"Oh—"

"He was telling us about the fifteen scalps he brought in the other day."

"Fifteen!"

"Isn't that right?"

"I don't recall the exact number."

"That was a good haul."

"Yes, but it does not happen often."

Flynn eyed him steadily. "I was wondering how often it does happen. This Lazair must be pretty good to take that many at one time. He only has about a dozen men."

"I suppose," Duro said, "he knows many tricks in the tracking of Indians."

"I suppose," Flynn said.

"Would you care for a drink?" Duro said now, looking from one to the other.

Flynn said, "Fine," and Bowers nodded.

Duro went into the next room and returned with the bottle of mescal and three tumblers. "I have this for special guests," he said confidingly.

Flynn watched him place the glasses on his desk and pour

mescal into them. "He had a Mimbre brave in his camp," he said.

Duro looked up. "This Lazair?"

Flynn nodded. "He'll be bringing you the scalp pretty soon."

"Oh . . . he was dead."

"He was after a while."

Duro shrugged. "Lazair is a businessman. A live Apache is worth nothing to him."

Bowers said quietly, "You get the feeling a live anything is worth nothing to him."

"Except perhaps a woman," Flynn added.

Duro handed them each a glass and said offhandedly, "He has a woman with him?"

"Didn't you know that?" Flynn asked.

"I have never visited his camp."

They sipped at the mescal, saying nothing. It was not a tension, but an uneasiness. After a moment Flynn said, "How do his men get on in the village?"

Duro shrugged. "As well as can be expected. They are, of course, sometimes primitive in their ways. As men would have to be who live as they do, by fighting Indians. But I have asked our people to treat them with courtesy since they are rendering our government a service." He sighed. "But sometimes they eye our women too covetously and with this my men are prone to raise objections."

"In other words," Flynn said, "they don't get along."

"Not all of the time, no."

"Lieutenant," Bowers said, "one of the reasons we came . . . I wonder if I could talk you into selling me a gun from your stores. I lost both of mine yesterday. That's if you have any extras."

"I could not possibly sell you one," Duro said stiffly, then smiled. "But I would be honored if you would select any gun you wish, as a gift."

They finished their drinks and descended to the equipment room. Bowers chose a Merrill carbine, and then a .44

Remington handgun which Duro insisted that he take. And though again he offered to pay for the arms, Lieutenant Lamas Duro would have none of this.

Flynn said, "Let us buy you a drink now."

But Duro refused painfully. "I'm sorry . . . a volume of paper work awaits me. You would not believe that only thirty men can do so much to expand the records." He bowed. "Perhaps another time."

They walked off towards Las Quince Letras, leading their horses, as Duro mounted the stairs.

"Well," Bowers said wearily, "what does he know?"

"One thing I'm willing to bet on," Flynn answered, "—the difference between a Mimbre and a Mexican scalp."

From the sunlight they entered the dimness of Las Quince Letras, Flynn half expecting to see Frank Rellis, half hoping and ready, but Rellis was not there though four Americans were toward the other end of the bar at a front table. Three girls were with them. They looked up as Flynn and Bowers moved to the bar. Here and there were men of the village, older men, sipping their wine or mescal slowly to make it last and they looked up only for a moment.

"Those four weren't at Lazair's camp," Bowers said. The men with the girls at their table were still looking toward them.

"No, I didn't see them," Flynn said. He held up two fingers to the mustached Mexican behind the bar and said, "Mescal." Then to Bowers, "Let's sit down."

They brought bottle and glasses with them to a table. Bowers poured the mescal and pushed a glass toward the cavalry scout. His eyes held on the sandy mustache, waiting for Flynn to say something. Bowers was in charge—that's what the orders read—but it wasn't that simple. Just putting a man in charge doesn't make it so. Bowers was realizing this.

He said finally, "Now what?"

Flynn was making a cigarette. He lighted it and blew smoke and through the smoke said, "I'm going back to Lazair's camp."

"When?"

"As soon as I see Hilario."

"Alone?"

"I think it would be better." Looking at Bowers he added, "If there are no objections."

"Of course not."

Flynn leaned closer. "Have you been figuring this?"

"How does it stand?"

"I know which is the worst now. I think Soldado is in second place, then the rurales."

Flynn added, "None very pleasant, and all of them hating each other. What does that suggest?"

"The obvious. Get them against each other."

"You want to work on it?"

"I'm not sure about going about it."

"Santana, Duro's sergeant, I think he's the one to start on. Tell him about all the Mexican girls in Lazair's camp. Concentrate on Santana. Make up whatever you like; whatever he wants to believe; something that would take time to prove."

"And Duro?"

Flynn said thoughtfully, "And Duro—He's in with Lazair, that stands to reason since he's paying for scalps he knows damn well aren't Apache. Santana against Duro . . . that makes sense . . . if you can work it."

Abruptly, seriously, Bowers said, "Why was I sent on this?"

"Somebody had to go."

"You told Deneen he should have picked a man with more experience."

"I shouldn't have said that."

"Why did he pick me?"

"I don't know. How well does he know you?"

"I met Deneen in Contention for the first time."

"Your dad was Division Commander over both of us in the war. Maybe you knew, Deneen was a captain then. I've known him off and on for thirteen years."

"Well?"

Flynn shrugged. "Maybe he admired your father so, he knew you'd make a good soldier."

Bowers glanced up from his mescal, but said nothing.

"Look, what difference does it make?" Flynn said. "We're here now."

"He dislikes you," Bowers said, glancing at him again. "That's apparent."

"You can't like everybody."

"It's more than that."

"Why not just think about the job you have to do?"

"All right."

Flynn finished the mescal in his glass and rose. "I'm going to see Hilario now. Look for me the day after tomorrow. But if I don't come then, wait a few more days before you do anything."

"You don't want me to go with you?"

"If it doesn't work with one, it wouldn't work with two."

"You make it sound like taking a walk in the park."

The corners of Flynn's eyes creased as he smiled; then the eyes were serious. "Look, I'd like to help you . . . but there isn't any pattern to these things. You can't open *Cooke's Cavalry Tactics* and get the answer. Much of this is patience. But having time to think, you end up worrying about what you're going to do first, then about why you were sent and you even worry whether or not Apaches become afraid." Flynn smiled. "I meant that as no offense."

Bowers said, "That's all right."

Flynn sat down again. "Let's get it out in plain sight. You know Deneen doesn't have one ounce of authority to send us down here?"

"He's Department Adjutant. I'd say that was enough."

"In Arizona. This is Mexico, somebody else's country. Remember, the orders said the army would not recognize us as lawful agents if we were held for any reason."

"He explained that to me in Contention," Bowers said. "He said so far it was a verbal agreement with Mexico. We can cross their border so many miles and they can enter the United States, if it means running down hostiles. He said he had to put that not responsible business in the orders as a formality. The agreement was supposed to be in writing soon, he said probably before we'd get here."

"But Duro said *if his government had known about it* . . ." Flynn said. "That doesn't sound like an agreement."

"Then why are we here?" Bowers said.

Flynn hesitated. "You're here because you're obeying an order." He added, "Because you're not in a position to question authority." Now go easy, he thought, and said, "I'm here because I want to be. It's that simple."

"Yet you say neither of us have any business being here." He wanted to ask Flynn what was between him and Deneen, but it wouldn't be in order.

Flynn smiled again. "All right, but what would you be doing if you weren't here? Parade drills . . . patrols that never find anything . . . mail-run escort—"

Bowers nodded.

"So . . . why don't we do the world a good turn and kick Soldado's Apache tail back to San Carlos. And if problems come along we'll meet them one at a time and not worry about everything at once. Right?"

Bowers nodded, thoughtfully. "All right." He watched Flynn rise and move to the door, then nodded as Flynn did. The screen banged.

He took a sip of the mescal and putting the glass down he saw the four Americans watching him.

The street of the house of Hilario Esteban was quiet. There were sounds from other streets, but here was only sun glare on sand-colored adobe and a thin shadow line close to the houses extending down both sides of the street. The bull-fight poster near the deserted home of Anastacio Esteban was hanging in small shreds now and only a few words were readable.

A small boy ran out of the house next to Hilario's.

"I will hold your horse!"

Flynn swung down and handed him the reins. "Carefully."

"With happiness," the boy smiled.

It was a woman who opened the door to his knock. Stooped, beyond middle age, a black scarf covered her shoulders and her dress beneath that was black. Hilario appeared behind her and his eyes brightened.

"Davíd!"

"How does it go?"

"Well," the alcalde answered. He motioned the woman and Flynn past him into the room.

The woman moved to the fireplace and sat on the floor there. She began stirring a bowl of atole and did not look at Flynn. With her head down, her figure was that of a child who weighed less than ninety pounds.

Hilario indicated the woman and said, "La Mosca. She is a herb woman, but now she prepares atole for me out of kindness. If there were a wound on my body, La Mosca would apply to it seeds of the guadalupana vine each marked with the image of the Virgin and soaked in mescal . . . or a brew of pulverized rattlesnake flesh if I were afflicted with the disease which the gachupines introduced to the women of our land . . . but she can do nothing for me now."

"Listen, Hilario," Flynn said. "I have not much time. I've come to tell you that your daughter is alive. I saw her."

He heard the soft rough sound that cloth makes and La Mosca, the curandera, was next to him.

"I have felt this," she said, "and have already told our alcalde of it."

Flynn said, "All right. Then I'm confirming what you have already told."

Hilario's voice was barely above a whisper, breathing the words in disbelief. "Is it true? Where?"

"If I told you that, you would go there hastily—"

"With all certainty!"

"And that would not be wise." He touched the old man's arm. "Look. I am going there now, with a plan. It is a matter of trusting me. If I told you where I was going perhaps others would find out—"

"Not from me."

"Perhaps not. But this not telling you is an additional safeguard."

The curandera said then, "She is being held by a man."

Hilario looked at her. "This comes to you?"

La Mosca nodded. "The man is not Indian. That I also know."

She can figure that out without looking into the future, Flynn thought.

"Is this true, Davíd?"

"My companion, the one I came with, will remain here. He knows about this and will help you if for a reason I cannot come back."

Quietly Hilario said, "All right."

La Mosca said now, "You will come back." Her wrinkled face looked up at Flynn. "This comes to me now. You will return by the beginning of *Día de los Muertos*—the festival of the dead—and you will bring with you the daughter of this man."

Thirteen

●

He studied the place for a long time, his gaze holding on the shape that was barely visible through the trees at the bottom of the shallow slope.

Someone was there. Not a movement, but something resembling a human form, though from this distance it was hard to tell. Flynn was on his stomach in the coarse grass that grew among the pines here. His horse was yards behind him, below the line of the hill.

Above the tree that he watched, a cliff rose shadowed with crevices and grotesque chimneys; pink cantera stone fading pale as the threat of rain washed the sky gray. High above the thickening clouds was an eruption of sunlight, a cold light that fanned upward away from the rain that was to come.

Minutes passed and the shape did not move.

Flynn eased back from the crest to his mount and pulled the Springfield from its scabbard. He crouched at the crest again studying the shape, then rose and moved slowly, cautiously down the slope into the trees.

There it was. And he saw now why there had been no movement.

It was Matagente. He was hanging from the

twisted limb of a juniper by a short length of rawhide that squeezed into the flesh of his throat. Matagente no longer wore his headband . . . the crown of his head had been hacked off for its scalp.

It's a warning, Flynn thought, meant for Soldado. But probably the buzzards would have found him before Soldado.

And then it occurred to him: But where are they? If there are no buzzards then he was just hung there . . . within the hour probably. Because Lazair shot him this morning you assumed he was put here then. But if he'd been here all day there wouldn't be much left of him—

He went back up the slope and returned to his mount, drawing a clasp knife from his pocket, and from the height of the McClellan saddle had to raise himself only a little more to reach the rawhide and cut it. He held the Apache about the body as he did this, feeling hard flesh and caked blood that crumbled against his hand and as he felt the full weight he tried to bend Matagente across the pommel of his saddle. But the body was stiff with death.

He used the rawhide line then, piecing it together, and dragged the Mimbre behind the horse carefully through the evergreens until he reached the sandy cantera cliff. There was no other way to do it.

He carried Matagente then, when he was closer to the wall, and laid his body into a hollow of the base. There were hundreds of cracks, hollows and niches here, sharply shadowed black seams rising with the heights of the pink façade. Then he placed rocks over the hollow and within minutes Matagente was a part of the cliff.

Flynn retraced his steps then, smoothing the marks Matagente's dragged body had made.

Let's go slow now, he told himself. Let's think it out before jumping into anything. Their camp is beyond the cliff and even up another climb farther on. If they were to ride to Soyopa they would pass this place. They could have hung him here on their way . . . but I would have seen them

. . . Not necessarily. You could have passed in timber. You could have missed them easily and there would not have been a dust rise in the trees.

He looked at the sky now. It's going to rain before dark. I can't picture Lazair's men riding out into the rain unless ordered to, unless he was there to make them.

Tracks. It occurred to him then. With the rain there will be no tracks tomorrow of where they went today. They can hang Matagente and Soldado cannot trace the sign to Lazair's camp.

He rode back to the juniper from which Matagente had been hanging and looked at the ground. The tracks, half-moon impressions of steel-shod hooves, went east . . . not to Soyopa, nor back to Lazair's camp. There had been no attempt to cover the tracks.

That's it, Flynn thought, they're counting on the rain. They're riding because it's going to rain and they're not going to all this trouble for anybody else but Soldado. Setting up an ambush at a logical place . . . along some trail they think the old Indian would have to take some time or another . . . and they don't want their tracks to warn him and turn the ambush around. And if this is true, then there would not be many at Lazair's camp now.

He went on, and even though he could feel an excitement inside of him now he traveled at the same careful pace, watching four directions as he skirted the steep slant of cliff wall and began climbing again, now into dwarf oaks. He would stop and wait and listen, then go on. You never knew for sure, so why take a chance?

Finally he reached the meadow and by this time it was beginning to drizzle. It was not yet dark and a gray mist hung over the sabaneta grass that would bend silently in a wave as the wind stirred. The rain made a sound, but it was a soft, hissing whisper that was not there after you listened to it long enough.

He would move when it was dark. He'd cross the meadow and climb the slope there two hundred yards away and find the guard before the guard found him. If the rain keeps up it will help, he thought.

Then he would find out if he'd guessed right. He had planned to watch here until the band of scalp hunters rode out . . . even if it might take a few days . . . but now he was almost certain they were not in camp, and waiting to make sure would only waste time.

It took longer for full darkness to creep over the meadow, because Flynn was waiting for it, but finally it settled and with it the rain seemed louder.

Pretend you're Mimbreño, he thought as he left the cover of the trees and started across the meadow. This would be easy for one of Soldado's boys. It would be nothing. But think of the guard now; he was up in the rocks before; that doesn't mean he'll be there now. It's raining. If he's taken cover you'll have to be careful; but at least he won't hear you with the rain. Think like an Apache. But don't kill him, he thought then. Not if you can help it.

Faintly he could see the shape of the rock rise against the sky. We were over more to the right, he thought, remembering the outline of the crest as it had looked to him the first time. The first and only time . . . this morning. And that's hard to believe that it was this morning. The guard had been to the left then. Now he would be directly in front of you if he's in the same place.

Flynn moved to the right, now, holding the detail of the rock rise in his memory and now estimating where the defile would be. He moved closer, threading into the rocks and there it was just above him slanting darkly into the slope.

He eased himself up over the rocks, crawled, lay flat to listen, then crawled again to the pass opening and rose, looking up to the ledge where the guard had been that morning.

He's not there. Flynn's gaze came back to the defile which was totally dark as far as he could see—*or* maybe he's in there using an overhang for shelter. But maybe there isn't any guard—and if there isn't, then you *know* Lazair's gone.

That's the way it would be—nobody bothering to take watch if Lazair wasn't there to make him.

But you have to be sure.

He moved in a little farther, listening. Then went the rest of the way through without hesitating, crouched low to one wall, and at the other end he went down into the wet grass, feeling it cold against his hands and face, and looked out at the camp.

Across the open area he could make out the horses. They had drifted into the aspens, and now he heard one of them whinny, a faint shrill sound in the darkness.

The rain made a splattering sound against the tents. The ties of one had unfastened and the flaps billowed and then popped as the wind rose to sweep stinging into the camp. Three of the tents were deserted. The fourth stood ghostlike in the darkness—a lantern inside illuminating the pale, wet canvas outline.

No light showed from the cave entrance.

A man's voice came from the lighted tent. The sound of a word, then laughter, faint sounds far away.

Flynn raised himself slowly and edged along the rock outcroppings that rimmed the pocket. Nearing the cave, a vertical crack of light now showed along one edge of the blanket that covered the entrance. And then he was up the slight rise under the shelter.

Now, very quietly, he thought. Take all the time you want because you'll do this just once. He put his hands into his coat and dried them against his shirt. He wiped his face with a bandana then drew his pistol and wiped it carefully.

The voice sound came from the tent again and Flynn could feel it inside of him tightening his chest. He pictured the men in the tent. He pictured four of them for some reason. I could go down there and empty this into the canvas and get all of them, he thought. Then: Don't be foolish. Come on now.

Cocking the pistol he brushed aside the blanket covering and the next moment was inside the cave—in high, room-size dimness, a line with clothes hanging from it, bedding along one wall, and in a corner, crouched beside the coal-oil lamp turned low, was Nita Esteban.

Flynn put one finger to his mouth. Then, "Don't speak out loud," he said softly.

The girl looked up at him, her body tensed. She was kneeling on a blanket, sitting back on her feet. Her hands held the blanket tightly and no part of her body moved.

Close to her, Flynn dropped to one knee. "Nita." He put his hand on her shoulder and took it away feeling her body shudder. "I'm not one of them." He touched her again, gently. "Do you remember, six months ago I came through Soyopa and stayed at the house of your uncle. I was a friend of his, *Davíd Flín.*"

Her eyes held his—searching, deep black eyes that were not sure. And then they were sure. Then they remembered and the dark eyes in the drawn face were suddenly glistening with tears. Flynn brought her to him gently and heard and felt the muffled sob against his chest. Her shoulders quivered and he held her close to him, awkwardly with one hand because the pistol was there, now moving the other hand up to stroke her hair, with much the same feeling you stroke a child's head.

Lowering his face he said to her ear, "How many are there?"

The sobbing stopped. "Most of them left during the afternoon. There would not be many now. One of them came here not long ago. I thought you were he when you entered."

"There is a light in only one tent."

"They are the only ones," she said. "Perhaps three, or four or five. The one who was here came for a bottle of something to drink." She hesitated. "He said I should go with him, but I refused and he said that when he came back I would be sorry."

Flynn rose, bringing her up with him. She wore a skirt to her ankles and a man's shirt buttoned high and the shirttail hanging to where her knees would be.

"Lazair keeps his clothes here, doesn't he?"

She nodded, but did not look at his face.

"Put another shirt on."

He moved to the blanket covering as she did this and stood listening. There it was again; one of them laughing. Then another sound—close!

He had time to warn the girl only with his eyes. She saw him flatten against the wall. A leather coat was hanging there from a nail and he drew the coat in front of him, though he still could be seen.

Then the blanket cover was whipped back and a man stood in the entrance, weaving, his eyes narrowing on Nita Esteban, then smiling.

"You must a been coming to see us. Nowhere else you could go." Mescal was in his voice and in the half-open eyes. He had come from the tent bareheaded and now his hair was shining, plastered close to his skull. He had brought no hat, but he was armed. He chuckled and turned to the wall where Lazair's gear was, where the mescal was kept.

He was about to say something more to the girl but the words caught in his mouth. He could see Flynn, and the pistol pointed toward him.

The man wheeled. In split-second surprise he wheeled toward the cave entrance.

Flynn held back, then there was no choice and he felt the .44 jerk with the exploding sound.

The scalp hunter stumbled, rolling to his side. His hand waved, slapped against his holster . . . the glint of metal coming up with the hand . . . then a second report, earsplitting in the closeness, and the man fell back and did not move.

They were over him, past him, almost the same moment. Flynn holding the girl's arm, brushing aside the blanket, then out into darkness running for the scattered rimrocks. And as they reached cover the other men were coming out of the tent, furiously at first—the canvas shaking, something kicked over, glass breaking, curses—then the light was extinguished and the men were outside. Now they made no sound. Now it was realization of what they had to do and they approached toward the cave slowly, fanning out, as Flynn and the girl crept to the defile and made their way through the blind narrowness of it.

There were four of them—it went through Flynn's mind— now only three, but you can count on them coming, coming quick!

His hand was tight clutching Nita's arm and he ran with her through the swishing wet sound of the sabaneta grass, holding himself to run at the girl's speed.

There was his mount, where he had left it. Hide glistening wet, skittering nervously at the abruptness of their coming into the trees. Flynn mounted, now reached for the girl and swung her up behind him and felt her arms holding as he wheeled the horse off through the trees. They descended, following the trail in his memory, crossed a flat stretch on the dead run then climbed again into timber before stopping to listen.

At first it was only the sound of Nita's breathing, then far off, faintly, he could hear the horses.

They're close, he thought, straining to listen, now conscious of his own breathing. They've figured it out. Somebody from Soyopa since it was not Apaches. So they're running hard in the direction of Soyopa. If they don't overtake someone they'll double back and in the morning spread out and start looking.

The sound of running horses was louder now. They had reached the flat stretch below them. Still mounted, unmoving, with the girl's arms tightening about him, they heard the horses pass, carrying their sound with them into the distance again. The girl's arms relaxed.

"We'll have to wait until it's light," Flynn said. "In the darkness we could run into them." He looked over his shoulder and saw her head nod.

Higher up in the timber they dismounted. Flynn kindled a low burning fire, without worrying about it being seen. A brush rimmed pocket shielded them on three sides. The fire might be visible from the fourth, but a man would have to be standing less than twenty feet away to see it and if he were that close, fire or no fire he'd know they were there.

They sat close over the mesquite twig fire letting their clothes dry on them. The girl's were not so wet, but Flynn's were stuck cold to his body and it was some time before the fire warmth penetrated enough for him to feel it on his body.

Later on, they lay close to each other to sleep.

"Nita."

The girl's face turned to his and was only a few inches away.

He said in Spanish, softly, "I offer my sorrow for what has happened, though the words do little good."

"There is nothing one can say," the girl answered.

"Your father is well."

"Will you take me to him?"

"Of course. When it is light. When we can go without the fear of coming onto those without seeing them."

She's calm, Flynn thought. Even after all she's been through she has control of herself and can speak without her voice giving it away. She's a woman of Mexico, used to the sight of death—but that's a lot of nonsense. No, it's not callousness. It's faith. God is God and He lets things happen and that's all there is to it. But He has reasons, and His reasons for something happening would be more important than a man's reason for questioning whatever it might be. That's how she has probably looked at it and it has taken some of the sting out. Not all, some.

Flynn said now, "I have thought of you often since the time in Soyopa."

Nita had closed her eyes. Now she opened them. "I remember you well. At first I did not, because in my mind I was expecting the other, but now I do."

He said abruptly, though gently, "Did Lazair cause you pain?"

"With his eyes," the girl answered. "He did not molest me

because he wanted me to consent. He would touch me, but that was all."

Flynn said, "I'm sorry," quietly, almost with embarrassment.

And then, as if they had been speaking of it before, the girl began: "The firing came suddenly from above, from both sides of the road and I saw my Uncle Anastacio fall from his horse. Others fell. There was screaming then and the mules began to go faster, but the wagons became entangled because the road was narrow and as this happened the men came down from the slopes firing their guns. One of them pulled me from the wagon and on the ground, beneath it, he tore open my dress and began to touch me, but the one called Lazair appeared and ordered him away. He took me up the slope to his horse and from there we watched what took place after"—she paused—"the scalping of those who had been killed, and some who had not been killed. Then he rode down the slope, holding me in front of him on the saddle, and ordered the men to cut loose the mules and burn the wagons. But after only two of them were burning he said to not bother with the others as it was time to go. Then four men rode through dragging saplings to obliterate the signs that were there. Then I saw one of my cousins being carried on another horse. She tore herself from the man who carried her and ran back toward the burning wagons, and the man shot her as she ran. One of those with the saplings dismounted and was drawing his knife as Lazair turned and rode off with me."

Nita said no more. She lay facing him, but her eyes were closed and her soft, shadowed features seemed relaxed now. Flynn put his arm around her gently. Through the night they lay close together and neither spoke again.

With first light they were moving down through the timber, through the gray mist that clung to the trees, left behind by night. Flynn carried the Springfield, leading the horse. Nita was mounted. Moving, winding slowly with the squeaking of straining leather and the crisp cracking rustling of hoofs in dried leaves.

Then they were crossing sand that muffled the hoofs; through mesquite and catclaw that tangled both sides of a draw, and there was ocotillo that yesterday had been thorned stalks but now blazed scarlet with the rain. The sky told there would be more rain and Flynn could smell it coming on the sultry wind.

The draw began to slope, gradually at its beginning, cutting between sweeping slopes, and as they followed the rise it narrowed, curving high up into the hills. In timber again, in the shadowy silence of it, they looked back down the way they had come. Far below, three riders were entering the draw.

They've found the tracks, Flynn thought. And now they know there are only two of us. One man and one woman. They probably aren't very worried and are thinking now it's getting interesting. He pictured them grinning at each other.

The girl had been watching them and now she looked at Flynn, asking the question with her eyes.

He said, "We can't run, because they can move faster. They would overtake us. The only thing to do is show them that we are aware of them and try to make them go slower." And he added, in his mind: Or stop them from going at all.

He moved the girl deeper into the trees then crept out among the rocks that overhung the steep-falling slope here. Dropping to his stomach he pushed the Springfield out between the rocks and looked down the barrel.

There they were, closer now, out of sight passing through jackpines, then reappearing. From his pocket Flynn brought out two brass cartridges and put them on the ground, on the spot where his hand would drop after swinging open the breech.

Five hundred yards, he thought. Take your time, they'll get closer. His eyes moved ahead of them, up the draw to where it narrowed and began to curve. But you'll have to hit them before they reach there. They'd have cover then and be able to sneak up through the brush if you miss with your first shot. So you'll fire from three hundred yards. It's a good thing it's downhill. They make them short in the barrel for shooting from horseback, but for long range you might just as well spit.

Now it was four hundred yards. They were single-file, taking their time.

Hit the first one. First things first. Let them get up to that open spot, so they won't be able to break for cover. But you won't get them all. You know that.

Close over the barrel he watched them come. The Springfield was cocked. His finger fondled the trigger lightly, feeling the spring tightness of it. The front sight covered the first rider. A little closer now, he thought.

All right.

His trigger hand tightened, squeezed closed. The shot rang, ripping thin air, echoing down canyon. The first horse was down. The man was on the ground. But now he was up, running. The second rider made a tight circle and leaned to help him up as the third one streaked away. He swung up behind the cantle and they were moving down the draw as Flynn fired again. The man went back, rolling off the horse's rump.

He threw open the breech and shoved in the third cartridge and fired as he lowered his head. The second horse went down. The rider hit and rolled and scrambled for cover. The third rider was out of range now.

Flynn looked back to the man he had hit. He was lying face-down. The other one was crawling toward him now. He knelt next to him and stayed there and Flynn thought: He must be alive.

Flynn had inserted another cartridge. He lowered his head, looking down the barrel at the man's back; then looked up again. He's got enough troubles now, Flynn thought, and backed away from the rocks.

They moved on through what was left of the morning, riding double now, running the horse when they would reach level stretches; but most of the time their travel was slow, following the maze of canyons and sweeping climbing draws that gouged the foothills, lacing in all directions. They bore a general direction west toward Soyopa, keeping the looming gray mass of the Sierra Madre behind them, the Mother Mountain that towered into the overcast sky losing her crested shapes gray against gray.

It was after noon, shortly after, when they stopped again, having come down into a ravine thick with aspen to a stream that was running with yesterday's rain.

When she had finished drinking, Nita Esteban sat on the grassy bank watching Flynn water the horse.

"We might reach Soyopa by nightfall," he said, looking toward her. Flynn spoke in Spanish. She had leaned back, resting on her arm. "You're tired, aren't you?"

"Knowing that we are going home takes much of the tiredness out of this."

She smiled then and Flynn thought, watching her: Now she's a girl again. This is the first time she's smiled. Before she was a woman. In her eyes the worn look of a woman who has seen an entire lifetime turn rotten. But now she's a girl again because she can look forward to something. Home.

"But from now on we'll have to use more caution."

She looked at him with surprise. "Those others are far behind."

"Two of them are. Perhaps all three, but we have no assurance of that. The third one is still mounted. He might have remained with his companions. He could be following us . . . or he might have circled to cut us off." He added gently, "I tell you this so you won't relax your guard entirely."

They moved on and it stayed in Flynn's mind now and he hoped the girl was thinking about it, being ready. The Springfield was across his lap and his gaze edged inching up over the brush on both sides of the ravine. The sides were steep and high up were pines. But being ready didn't lessen the shock when it came.

The shot broke the stillness, coming from nowhere. It ricocheted off rock above their heads, whining into the air. The second shot hit lower, but they were off the horse then, Flynn pushing the girl, running crouched, jerking the horse after them. Two shots followed them to cover and then stillness again.

Why didn't he wait, Flynn thought. Maybe he's jumpy. Or else that was his best shot and he took it. If it was he couldn't be closer than a hundred yards. He leaned close to Nita.

"He fired from the left slope, high up."

She waited for him to say more, her eyes wide, the pupils dilated an intense black.

"He has us . . . until we find him." He said then, "Do you know how to fire this?" handing her the Springfield.

"Once I did, but it was long ago."

He pointed it out in front of her and cocked it. "All you do is pull the trigger now. But don't fire unless he is close . . . if he should come. Keep it low; then if he should come onto you, wait until he is from here to there"—he pointed out just beyond the rocks—"then fire."

He moved quickly then, surprising the girl; up over the rocks, through the brush into the open; the sound of his running across the ravine, then a bullet spanged kicking dust behind him; his head was up watching for it and there it was, the almost transparent dissolving puff of powder smoke high up, farther down. Then he was into the brush going up the slope.

Now you know, Flynn told himself. But so does he.

At the top he kept to the pines, making a wide circle to where the scalp hunter would be. Three times he stopped to listen, but there was no sound. He went on, inching into the rocks. There was his horse! Then it would be close, right ahead, he thought, looking up beyond and back along the ravine. He moved closer, cautiously, with the pistol in front of him. There—

Three cigarette stubs. Boot scuff marks in the sand. But he's gone—

Flynn was over the rocks, scrambling down the brush slope, sliding with the shale that crumbled under his boots; at the bottom he crouched, hesitated, then started back to where Nita was, quickly, keeping to cover. And he saw the man before he was halfway.

The scalp hunter was moving in a crouch, half crawling up the ravine. Now he straightened, bringing up a Winchester, and walked slowly toward the rocks where Nita was hidden.

Flynn raised the pistol, aiming—two hundred feet at least, that's too far—then beyond the man's shoulder something else, a movement. It was Nita. He could see her head, now her shoulders, and suddenly the scalp hunter was running toward her. He was almost to the rocks, almost to Nita, when he stopped in his stride and hung there as a thin report flattened and died. He fell then, rolling on his back.

Nita still held the Springfield, looking at the man she had shot.

"It's over now," Flynn said gently, taking the carbine from her. He looked at the scalp hunter, recognizing him as the one Lazair had called Sid. The red-bearded one who had had his pistol. Sid stared back at him with the whites of his eyes and his jaw hung open in astonishment, though he had died the moment the bullet struck his chest.

They did not halt at dusk to make camp but went on, making better time now that both were mounted. Still, it was after midnight when they passed the cemetery and rode into the deep shadow of Santo Tomás.

A much smaller shadow glided out from the steps of the church as they came in the square. A woman. The face of La Mosca looked up at them from the blackness of the shawl covering her head.

"Man, it is as I said. You have returned. And now commences The Day of the Dead—"

Fourteen

●

Mescal, like tequila, is a juice of the maguey. As colorless as water unless orange peelings or pieces of raw chicken are dropped in while it's standing. When you see mescal a rich yellow, you'll know that's what it is, chicken or orange peels.

Who told him that? A straining, groaning authoritative voice in a stagecoach trying to outshout axles that hadn't taken grease in forty miles of alkali . . . coming into somewhere.

Lieutenant Regis Duane Bowers poured himself another drink.

He drank well, because he had a good stomach; though he would have tried to drink as much if he didn't have a stomach, because it was part of being a cavalryman. You can tell a cavalryman by his walk and the way he wears his kepi and by the amount of whisky he can drink like a gentleman. These as much a part of being cavalry as a saber.

Now he was sitting. He wore neither kepi nor saber. And he was drinking mescal. It doesn't matter. It's something inside. Those things help: a slanted kepi and a saber, but they are only badges; you are a cavalryman because you think like one and feel like one and then you know

you're one. That's all. Just one of those things you know
. . . and don't let anybody say different.

One of the Mexican girls was looking at him now, a smile
softening her mouth as he glanced at her. She was at the
table with the four Americans.

His eyes lowered and he sipped at the sweet liquor. There
was a lot to think about. But Flynn makes everything sound
simple. He looks at things in their proper perspective, things
one at a time, and doesn't worry about something that's supposed to happen next week because there's no assurance
there will be a next week. That's a good way to look at
things, but it takes some doing. Saying, well, we're here; we
might as well do the job. That's the easy way to look at
things. No it isn't. It's the hard way . . . when you don't
have any business being here. If what he says is true, it's
natural to want to go back to Deneen and tell him to go to
hell and next time find some authority. Staying on anyway
takes humility, doesn't it? It takes something. Something
that wasn't handed out with *Cavalry Tactics*. But that's as-
suming Deneen doesn't have the authority, and you don't
assume anything.

Flynn can almost convince you that he's right even before
he says one word. It's his manner. The way he goes about
things. He doesn't get excited. He seems absolutely perfectly
honest with himself; that's why you believe what he says.
After being with him only a few days part of him rubs off.
The feeling you've known him a long time. Relaxing. Maybe
he's right about Deneen overstepping his bounds . . .

Don't get carried away. Maybe he is; and maybe he isn't.
Remember, you're talking about a colonel with fifteen years
and a war behind him. They don't generally make mistakes
like that. There's something between him and Flynn, something personal, so naturally Flynn is against him. But I'm
glad Flynn's here. He speaks quietly and sometimes you get
the idea he's lazy and doesn't care, but I wouldn't want to be
fighting against him.

He wanted to be a good friend of Dave Flynn's, and often

since leaving Contention, he wondered if Flynn ever thought about their first meeting, at the cavalry post before Deneen came in. He had been aloof then, maybe snobbish in Flynn's eyes. It bothered him, because he hadn't meant to seem a snob. It was just that he wanted to show them he wasn't a kid, that he knew what it was all about. He wanted Flynn's respect . . . even if he wasn't sure how right Flynn was about Deneen's authority.

He noticed the Mexican girl get up: the one who had been watching him. The man next to her said something and put his hand on her arm, but she jerked away from his grasp and the next moment was coming toward Bowers.

"May I sit with you?"

Bowers half rose, self-consciously, glancing at the other table. Then: The hell with them. She can go wherever she wants. They don't own her.

"I am enchanted."

She smiled. "You speak our language well."

"That was only a word."

"Now you've said five, equally well."

Bowers smiled. "I have learned in the past year to understand some of what is said, but it is yet difficult to speak. Most of the words I don't yet know."

"You need someone to accompany you, to make interpretations." She looked at him slyly from under dark lashes and smiled.

"I would never learn the language that way."

"Perhaps you would learn other things."

He felt them looking at him. "What about your friend?"

She glanced coldly over her shoulder. "He is not my friend; nor any of them there. I amuse myself with them only." Her glance returned quickly as one of the men rose and came toward their table.

It was Lew Embree. He bumped the next table unsteadily. A two days' beard growth darkened his face; mescal showed in his glazed, watery eyes and in the way his mouth was parted, sticky wet in the corners, loose in his bearded jaw.

The girl refused to look at him.

"Honey, I didn't come to see you, but your friend. When I come for you you'll know it." The sleepy eyes went to Bowers.

"I wondered if you knew your friend Frank was here?"

Bowers hesitated. "Frank who?"

"Frank Rellis."

"I don't know anyone by that name." But he remembered it. As he said it he pictured the two riders through the field glasses and the one on the left with the Winchester; then tying that in with what Flynn had told him before. Frank Rellis. The man who shot Joe Madora. Then Lazair mentioning him.

"Frank told how he knew you and your partner. In Contention, as I recollect."

"I've never met Frank Rellis."

The girl pretended to shudder and shook her head. "That one!"

"Well, he says he knew you and your partner."

"He must be mistaken."

"Frank doesn't say much, so when he does it's something he's sure of 'cause he's had all that silent time to think about it."

"If he's not mistaken then you misunderstood what he said."

"I heard him plain as your face tell Curt that he knew you."

Bowers said nothing and looked at his glass.

"He's over eatin'. He'll be back shortly; why'nt you wait to see him?"

"If I'm still here when he comes then most likely I'll see him."

"He said it was in Contention—"

"Look, I've never met Frank Rellis!" He looked at the man steadily now wondering if he was really drunk, even though it was on his face. The girl was suddenly looking beyond him and now he heard the door and the ching of heavy Mexican spurs. Sergeant Santana stopped at the bar.

Lew Embree looked at him a long moment and then glanced at the girl. "Come on, honey."

"I like it where I am."

"You be nice now."

"Go stick your head in it!"

"Honey, Warren's back there at the table cryin' his eyes out for you."

The girl did not say anything now.

Shaking his head Lew Embree looked at Bowers. "Don't these biddy-bitches get uppity though. She suspects you got more money than Warren, which could be a case." He was standing next to her chair. His hand moved to the cane back rest then idly up to the girl's neck, and suddenly, his fingers gripping the white cotton, he jerked his hand down, ripping the loose-fitting blouse away from her back. She was up out of the chair, screaming, holding the front of the blouse to her breasts, running toward the rear of the mescal shop, past the table where Warren and the others were, trying to dodge an arm that reached for her and caught a shred of material. It pulled her off balance, jerking the front of the blouse from her hands and now she made no attempt to cover herself, standing, cursing Embree with every indecent word she knew before running crying through the rear door.

Warren called to Lew, "She looks like she can't hardly wait!"

Still grinning, Lew Embree looked from Santana to Bowers then turned his back to them indifferently and started for the other table. "For a girl that throws it around like she does," Lew was saying, "she acts awful kittenish."

Bowers watched Embree until he reached the other table, then he looked toward Santana.

"Will you sit here?"

The rurale sergeant pushed back his straw Chihuahua hat, shaking his head faintly. "I will be here only a moment."

Bowers stood and moved to the bar carrying the mescal

bottle. "Let me buy you a drink." He said then, "I was wondering what that man's name was."

Santana accepted the bottle that Bowers extended and poured a glass half full. "I've never listened for his name."

"That was something he did to the girl, eh?"

"She had her clothes off in his presence before."

"I had the feeling he did it for my benefit," Bowers said, watching the rurale.

Santana shrugged, then drank. He wiped his mouth and said, "He misses no opportunity to show they have bought these women well. But it makes little difference since the women *are* bought; it's hardly a winning of their affection."

Bowers said idly, "But it would seem to me to be a matter of principle. I don't know if I could just let these men come in and take over all the women. That's if it was up to me."

Santana was watching the ones at the table. "This is not something that will go on always."

"I should think you'd have enough men that you wouldn't have to stand for such nonsense going on. Those are Lazair's men, aren't they?"

Santana nodded.

"Then you must have about three to one on him."

"We have been instructed to treat him with courtesy."

Bowers half smiled. "Where do you draw the line? If a guest at your home made advances to your wife, would courtesy hold you back from dealing with him?"

"There is a difference."

"You live in Soyopa. The women are yours, of your land. Then these come and take whatever they like and make themselves comfortable. Was it your lieutenant who said this about courtesy?"

Santana nodded. "That one."

"He hasn't been to Lazair's camp, has he?"

"No."

"I'm told there were some women there. Not like the ones that work here, but good girls, from another pueblo. Alaejos, somewhere like that. What they were doing to them I've heard called many things . . . but courtesy wasn't one of them."

"Where did you hear this?"

"From one of the men of the village. Now I'm not sure, that might have been a time ago and now they are gone."

Santana sipped his mescal; he was thinking, and it was even something physical, tightening his swarthy face. His eyes were small in his face and now they did not show as he squinted to make things plainer in his mind.

"When I heard that," Bowers said, "I couldn't help but be angry myself; but one man cannot do anything against all of them."

"What of your companion?"

"That would make two of us."

"No, I meant where is he?"

Bowers shrugged. "Probably at the house of the alcalde, or visiting others. He also cannot understand this immunity that seems to have been granted them."

"Lieutenant Duro—"

"Yes, Lieutenant Duro . . . who is forced to associate with them only when paying the scalp bounty. The rest of the time he is alone in his comfortable house with little to do—"

"Not always alone."

"But while you perform his work. I have heard that," Bowers said.

"What?"

"Everyone speaks of it. You're modest. It's said about that Duro would accomplish nothing if it were not for Sergeant Santana."

"That is said?"

"You are modest; for you know this better than I. How often does he come from his house into the sun?"

"Little."

"Perhaps for pleasure, but never for work, eh?"

Santana nodded, thoughtfully.

"It seems such a waste. Yet he is the one who insists that

you be courteous to the men of Lazair. Has he led you against the Apaches?"

"That one? That son of the great whore would sooner cut his arm off."

Bowers said, sympathetically, "You can find little respect for a man like that."

"None. Just the sight of him is an abuse."

Bowers said nothing, watching him.

Santana said, "In the army it isn't uncommon to find men such as he. I know that for I have served. As a boy I was present at the battle of Cinco de Mayo, where at Puebla, under Zaragoza and this same Diaz we now have, we defeated the army of France."

"That was a long time ago."

"Fifteen years," Santana answered. "But with the clearness of yesterday in my mind."

"And you have served all of this time?"

"Most of it."

"I didn't know you were a veteran of such long service."

"But this is not the army," Santana said.

"More a police force?"

"More an association of bandits. Listen . . . almost every one of my men has lived his entire life outside of the law. These you meet in all armies, but not in such proportion as here. To organize this, Diaz must have thrown open the jails."

"Then there is a problem making them obey orders."

"Listen." Santana looked at Bowers intently. "There is no problem. These that were conceived in stables and have seasoned in prisons . . . there is not one of them I cannot handle. If it were not for that pimp of a lieutenant, much more would be accomplished here. Lieutenant Duro sometimes believes he is much man, but it is only his rank that tells him so. Inside of him live worms."

Bowers shook his head. "That's too bad. Here you are, a military man, years of experience and with a force you could probably turn into a fine fighting corps . . . and they saddle you with an officer who has no feeling for service. I would venture that you could have taken your men even against this Soldado Viejo long before this if it were not for Duro."

"With certainty, even though they are not trained properly for the fighting of Indians; that is, as a body, which is the only way to defeat them."

"Taking them into the hills after Soldado would not be wise then."

"No. We have not been given trackers. How would we find them? And if we did, how would we assault them? Firing, puffs of the powder smoke high up, but when you climb to the place, nothing. Then you carry down your dead. It is always thus with the Apaches."

"But to get them in the open, eh?" Bowers prompted. He pushed the mescal bottle toward Santana, watching the sergeant light a cigar, puff hard, hurrying to light it.

"Aiii—to get them in the open. Listen, when that day comes we will flood them; we will sweep through their ranks and you will see riding you thought was not possible. There are many vaqueros among us; these will sweep them, firing, stinging like a thousand ants, then roping them to be dragged behind the horses. Then, instead of scalps, we will take the entire heads and secure them to poles and place each pole a certain distance apart, all the way to Hermosillo."

"If you get them in the open."

"Yes." Santana's voice was lower, the word part of his breath. Then he said, again excitedly, "Listen, tomorrow with the sun I am taking a patrol toward the pueblo of Alaejos. That is a good direction for Apaches. You come with us. Then, if we see Apaches down from the hills, I'll show you something, man, to tell them back home."

"How long would we be gone?"

"We would return the following day . . . in time for the fiesta. *Día de los Muertos*—"

Santana took one more drink, repeating that he had only a moment, then left the mescal shop.

Red Bowers exhaled slowly, a long sigh. Flynn had it right, Bowers thought. Santana arouses easily, and he hates Lazair's men. This could be all right. This could work, if it's handled properly. Just take it slowly. This could be like war from a general's saddle—moving troops, but only hearing the gunfire in the distance. Here's some practice for you. And then there's Duro . . . something for his ear.

He paid the bartender and started for the door.

"Boy . . . you goin' to wait for Frank!"

Bowers glanced back at the table where Embree and the other sat. He hesitated, then went out without bothering to answer.

He crossed the square towards Duro's house, leading his mount, hoofs clopping behind and a thin shadow with legs twice as long as they should be. The square was still vacant; the two rurales who had been in front of Duro's were not in sight.

He mounted the stairs heavily, slowly. If he were interrupting anything Duro would hear him and have time to clear away whatever it, or she, might be. That was the gentlemanly thing to do. But when he reached the veranda there was no sound from within. He called the lieutenant's name through the partly opened door. He waited, then pushed in when there was no answer. Calling again, he moved to the bedroom doorway—

Duro was on the bed, sprawled on his back. A fly buzzed close to his face, close to his open mouth. The mescal bottle was on the floor, but Duro still clutched the glass he'd been holding when he passed out.

"Officer and gentleman," Bowers said half aloud. He left then.

Lazair counted the scalps again as they returned to camp. He knew there were eight, but there was no harm in a recount. His hunch had paid off. With the rain the streams had filled. He had located his men at three watering places on the chance Soldado's people would come to one of them. And they had.

The second evening they came—seven women and two old men to protect them. And now they had eight scalps. One woman had gotten away. It was almost dark, but best to return to camp now than wait for a war party to come storming back for revenge. You could always pick off a few if you found the right water holes, that was the way to do it; but God, don't try and hit the whole bunch!

He'd sent a man to gather the ones at the other two places, and some men were bringing up the rear to cover sign as best they could in the fast-falling dark. Well, it was a worthwhile two days. He'd get a good rest, maybe have a little talk with Nita, and take the scalps in in the morning. A good day to go to town . . . there was supposed to be some kind of fiesta.

Fifteen
●

We are all afraid of death, Lamas Duro thought, but one admits it only to himself. He was standing on the veranda of his headquarters, watching the straggle of villagers coming now and then from the side streets, crossing the square in the direction of the cemetery.

In company we can be brave. We proclaim this festival, *Día de Los Muertos,* to celebrate on the grave stones and joke at death and tell him we aren't afraid . . . but these are only outward signs. With some of the people it takes a full bottle of mescal before they are at ease in his presence. And with others it takes even more. And he thought: Like yourself . . . it takes a bottle every day. Did you know that? For you, every day is *Días de Los Muertos.*

Looking across the square, he watched one group pass into the midmorning shadow of the church. They moved along the west wall, carrying their homemade wine and mescal, and lunches of bread—small loaves baked in the shapes of death's heads for the occasion.

Take a bite of death on the grave of your father.

Death and the devil are one. Show him you aren't afraid and he'll stay in hell where he belongs. But take another drink before it wears off and he comes leaping out.

Lamas Duro smiled. Children of the ignorant whore Superstition. But he thought: You believe in nothing, now; yet you conduct yourself in this manner every day. What does it mean?

He looked out over the square, at the shadow of the obelisk which was the only thing about the square that ever changed, and made the scene seem more monotonous because the change itself was a dull, inching thing that wasn't worth thinking about.

It means you're sick of life . . . but afraid of death, so you take the in-between, and that's mescal. You didn't begin that way. Even a year ago there was no fear, but that was before Diaz . . . and his rurales . . . his bandits, which is what they are.

It came suddenly, and he wasn't aware of the reason—though it must have been the picture of himself as he had once been, for that flashed in his mind, differently than it had the many times before, for consciously now he saw himself as he had been and, at the same time, as he was now—and he knew then that he would leave.

And the plan of what he would do fell into place quickly . . . remembering the bounty money in his possession and Lazair away from the pueblo and Santana due in from patrol that morning but being weary would be in the mescal shop or at camp and the entire population of Soyopa celebrating *Día de Los Muertos*. . . . No one, no one would notice a lone rider leaving Soyopa!

He would ride north . . . across the border. That was it. Living among the Americans would be something to get used to, but at least the bounty money would make the getting used to it less unbearable. And it now seemed so simple, so elementary, that he wondered why it had not occurred to him before this. He inhaled deeply, feeling his shirt tighten against his chest, then moved away from the veranda railing and went into the office.

A half-full mescal bottle that he had started only that morning was on the desk. He picked it up by the neck and was smiling as his arm swung wide and let it go. The bottle smashed against the far wall—shattering, flying glass and the liquid burst of it beginning to run down to the floor.

Entering the square, Bowers glanced at Santana. "What was that?"

Santana smiled through the sweat-streaked dust on his face. "This is a feast day. Many bottles are opened, some of them are dropped."

They were passing Duro's house, less than a hundred feet away, and nodding toward it Bowers said, "Sounded like it came from there."

Santana answered, "Lieutenant Duro has never dropped a bottle in the entirety of his life."

They stopped in front of Las Quince Letras, Bowers and Santana, with a few of the rurales pulling even with them now. Most of the rurales had swerved from the square down the street leading to their camp.

Bowers came off the saddle stiff-legged. It seemed a long time since dawn; riding steadily for hours with nothing happening made it seem like days. There were no Apaches, not even a pony sign all day yesterday or that morning. But the thought was in Bowers' mind all during the patrol that probably it was just as well. Santana wouldn't have been ready for Apaches had they appeared. He allowed his patrol to stretch thin. There was more than just talking in ranks—loud laughter, even drinking. Almost, it seemed to Bowers, as if their purpose was to ride through the brush to flush out game for a hunting party ahead. Santana failed to send out flankers. He kept two men riding advance, but each time the twenty-man patrol caught up with them they were dismounted, lying in the shade, if there was shade, or else with sombreros tilted over their faces. When they reached Alaejos, two men were missing. The two straggled in almost an hour later, and Santana said nothing to them. In more than a dozen places along the way, three Apaches could have annihilated a good half of the patrol. Bowers kept his thoughts to himself. By the time they had reached Alaejos, that afternoon, he realized it wasn't a lack of discipline; Santana didn't know what he was doing . . . in spite of his years in the army. He thinks he's a soldier, Bowers had thought, but he isn't even close to being one.

When they left Alaejos, a man in white peon clothes was with them. He rode between two rurales and his hands were tied to the saddle horn. A middle-aged man with tired eyes that looked at nothing. Santana said he was a thief and one purpose of the patrol was to bring him back to Soyopa to be tried by Duro. "What did he steal? I don't know. What difference does it make? I have the name and this is the man who answers to it."

A few miles out of Alaejos Bowers noticed Santana nod to one of the men next to the peon. The rurale dropped back half a length and suddenly slapped the peon's mount across the rump. Santana waited, deliberately. No one had moved. Bowers looked at Santana quickly, with astonishment that turned to shock as Santana smiled, waiting, then with the smile in the tone of his voice shouted for his men to stop him.

A dozen rurales fired, and when the man was on the ground motionless some of them were still firing.

"Why do they always try to escape?" Santana had said, then shrugged. "Ley fuga. It saves the cost of a trial."

They had made camp later on and started for Soyopa again with the first light.

Now it was midmorning as they entered Las Quince Letras.

"Mescal?" Santana asked, and when Bowers nodded he said, "This time on me."

Bowers waited as Santana paid for the bottle. He was more than a little tired of Santana now, after a full day and a half of him, but if he wanted to buy a drink that was all right. After, he would go to Hilario's house and wait for Flynn. Today was supposed to be the day.

He was surprised at the amount of people in the shop and then he remembered that this was a festival day. There was a hum of talking spotted with laughter and the sounds of glasses and bottles. And going over the room his eyes hesitated on the table where the four Americans sat. The same table as before. One of them was the man who had torn the girl's dress off. God, he must live here. And with the same three friends. No, one of them wasn't here the other day. His eyes moved on and came back to the bar and Santana was coming toward him with bottle and glasses. There was a vacant table in front of them and they sat down at it.

"Good crowd," Bowers said, "for before noon."

Santana smiled. "Preparing themselves for the graves."

"Part of the festival?"

"The big part. *Día de Los Muertos* lasts these three days. On this the first day, the graves of ancestors are visited. They are mourned, toasted and finally eaten over before the day is through. By the third day death is convinced that we aren't afraid of him."

Now they did not speak. As if there was nothing more in common between them which they had not already spoken of. Bowers, out of politeness, thought for something to say, but the things that occurred to him weren't worth talking about. There was the mescal to drink and many faces about and movements in the room to attract attention, so talk wasn't necessary. Bowers sank back into the cane-bottomed chair and sipped the sweet liquor, now and then thinking about the peon. "Why do they always try to escape?" Santana had said that, smiling. Bowers thought: If they were going to hang the man anyway, what difference does it make? But it did make a difference. It didn't seem right. Two men and a girl laughing at the next table and the girl saying something as she laughed, a phrase she repeated three, four times. The words had almost a musical sound and Bowers repeated the phrase in his mind trying to translate it. It's an idiom that you can't translate word for word. You have to concentrate, pick up the idioms, if you get those you've got the language. There's no reason in the world why you should think that peon was treated unfairly. He was a thief. He would have been tried and hanged. Their justice is somewhat more harsh, and they cut corners administering it. Now he heard the girl's voice at the next table again. He glanced that way, but a man's legs and stomach and chest were there. Two, three feet away, standing, and now Bowers looked up at him, recognizing the new man he had seen at the Americans' table and at the same quick moment he knew who the man was . . . though the first and only time he had seen him had been through field glasses focused on the man's back as he rode out of the canyon shadow.

"Where's your partner?" Frank Rellis said.

Bowers shrugged. "I don't know."

"Why don't you know?"

Bowers hesitated. "That's a funny question."

"I don't see anybody laughin'."

Bowers sat up straighter, slowly. "I said before I don't know where he is. I don't see how I can help you."

Rellis was holding a glass in his left hand. He raised it, finishing what he was drinking, then moved to the bar and brought the glass down hard on the polished surface. He was half watching Bowers as he did this and now he turned, leaning his elbows on the bar behind him. He stared for long seconds, staying in this position, motionless but relaxed, then he stirred. He began making a cigarette. Behind him, the bartender filled his glass with mescal. Rellis was hatless, hair hanging low on his forehead, and he needed a shave. It was evident that he had been drinking most of the morning: it showed in his eyes, though not in his voice. He was armed: a pistol hanging low on his right hip.

Rellis said, "You shouldn't a let him out of your sight. He probably run for home."

Bowers had looked away. Now his eyes returned to Rellis. "I'm not worried about that."

"What are you worried about?"

"Nothing."

"Does your partner know I'm here?"

Bowers shrugged. "I don't even know your name."

"Frank Rellis."

Bowers waited. "That doesn't mean anything to me."

"He never mentioned my name to you?"

"Why should he?"

"You're a goddamn liar if you say he hasn't."

It was in Rellis' mind, planted firmly, that Flynn was in Soyopa because he had followed him down after what happened in Contention, somehow learning of his having joined Lazair. Two men coming down to locate Soldado and his band made no sense at all. That was a cover-up. Lazair had a mule's ass for brains if he believed that. Rellis turned sideways to the bar and drank off part of the mescal.

It was going through his mind that this couldn't be better: the shavetail coming in alone . . . don't count the rurale . . . yeah, that was all right, too. Teach him a lesson he won't forget.

Bowers could see it. The tone of Rellis' voice and the right hand hanging free. He was angry, watching Rellis, seeing what he was doing, but he knew it was exactly what Rellis wanted. Jump up, drawing, at an insult . . . and not having a chance . . . so he sat still and let the anger start to pass off. His own pistol was wedged between his thigh and the chair arm rest, and the holster flap was snapped. And you had to miss the table edge bringing up the gun. Rellis has done this before, you haven't. The objections were there to calm him, to make him go slow, but they brought with them a fear, a small nervous fear, and planted it in the pit of his stomach.

His voice sounded loud in his ears as he said to Rellis, "I don't keep tab on him. If you want him, go out and start looking."

Rellis dragged on his cigarette and blew the smoke out slowly.

"What's your name?"

"Bowers."

"Bowers what?"

"Lieutenant Bowers."

Rellis' lips curled, grinning. "Well goddamn . . ." He said then, still grinning, "I was looking for you the other day. I came back from eatin' and they said you'd run off."

"You mean I'd left."

"You heard what I said."

"Why would I run away from you?"

Rellis lowered his head and drew on the cigarette, not taking his elbow from the bar. His head raised and the fingers holding the cigarette flicked out. The cigarette shot in a low arc and landed on the table in front of Bowers.

Bowers' eyes held on the man, feeling the heat on his face, wanting to do something, but . . . he was conscious of stillness . . . a sound close to him then: Santana mumbling an obscenity in his breath . . . and the sound of the screen door closing, but not seeing anyone come in because his eyes were on Rellis and Rellis, elbow on the bar, his hand hanging limp above his pistol butt, was returning the stare.

"Mostly," Rellis said now, "when I see a piss-ant like you I just step on him."

"Rellis—" It came unexpectedly, but without alarm.

Bowers' face relaxed, that was the effect, that suddenly, even without looking. But Rellis had to turn his head, sharply, and as he did the grin died on his face.

Flynn stood in from the doorway. He came on a few strides and stopped, his eyes on Rellis, his right hand unbuttoning his coat.

"Frank, I understand you've been looking for me."

Rellis wasn't loose now, though he was in the same position, elbows on the bar. Now he might have been nailed there.

"I . . . was just asking where you were."

"I heard you asking."

"Listen." Rellis straightened. "I want to get clear with you what happened in Contention. I might have talked out of turn in that barbershop—I'd been drinking and was anxious to ride out." He added quickly, "And that's what I did right after. I rode out a long ways to let my head clear, then camped by water and slept from early right through the night."

"And now you want to buy me a drink."

"That's right."

"You want to drink to what happened at the livery."

"Listen, I didn't have any part of that."

"What?"

"Shootin' that man."

"If you left Contention, how did you know about it?"

"News travels."

"All the way to Sonora?"

"It don't take long."

"Frank," Flynn said quietly, "you're a liar."

"You got no cause to say that."

Flynn moved toward Rellis. "It's said." He paused, watching Rellis' eyes. "I'm going outside. I'll expect to see you within the next few minutes . . . with your gun in your hand."

Rellis' face was stiff. Then it smiled, forcing the smile wide. "Now wait a minute. You're jumping to conclusions. I swear to God I wasn't near that livery!"

Flynn's eyes stayed on Rellis, though he did not speak. He stared, watching Rellis trying to appear unconcerned, and he became more confident because he knew then that Rellis was half afraid to fight. Rellis would bully Bowers, he thought, because Bowers was young, too new to have experience. Maybe Red could take him with his fists, but he wouldn't have gotten all the way out of the chair to try. This was different. This was something Rellis would want his own way or not at all, and Flynn thought: And you know how that would be. All right, let him have his way. Give him his chance.

He moved toward Rellis until only a stride separated them and suddenly, abruptly, he swung a fist up hard against Rellis' jaw. A brittle smacking sound, boot scuffing, Rellis hitting the bar, sliding back off balance, but not going down. An arm caught the bar edge. The hand moved down, but jerked back and he hung there, breathing with his mouth open, watching Flynn.

"I'll say it once more," Flynn said. "You're a liar. If you don't come out in five minutes I'll come back inside to kill you."

Flynn turned and moved toward the door. Now it's coming. Wait for Bowers. He was tensed. You'll hear it. One word. One word is all it will be and . . .

"Dave!"

He wheeled, drawing, thumbing the hammer, aiming with his eyes, firing. He fired once.

Rellis went to his knees, holding his chest, the uncocked pistol dropping from his other hand and he was dead as his face struck the floor.

Sixteen

●

Lew Embree placed his palms flat on the table, looking past Warren who was too drunk to know what had happened; then Lew pushed his weight on his hands, rising unsteadily. He moved between the tables, chairs scraping in the semi-stillness to make way for him, and when he stopped he was looking down at Frank Rellis.

Flynn's pistol pointed at Lew momentarily as he slipped it into the shoulder holster. "Take your friend out of here," Flynn said.

Embree looked up. "He's no friend of mine."

"Take him out anyway."

Embree shrugged. "If you hadn't done that, somebody else would've. The only trouble is somebody's got to bury the son of a bitch."

"You've buried men before, haven't you?"

Embree looked up again. "Sure."

"Then no one has to tell you how."

Flynn looked at Bowers who was next to him now. He motioned Bowers ahead of him and they went out of the mescal shop, then along the adobe fronts toward Hilario's street, Bowers leading his horse.

"I'm glad that's over," Flynn said. "It was one of those things that had to come and now I'm glad it's over with."

"It took some nerve to do it that way," Bowers said.

Flynn glanced at him, the smile at the corners of his eyes. "Red, I was counting on you for the signal."

"What if I'd been looking the other way?"

Flynn hesitated. "You can't think of everything at once." He said then, "How did you make out with Santana?"

"He's no soldier," Bowers answered. "He doesn't know the first thing about conducting a patrol . . . but he hates the bounty hunters. And he hates Duro even more."

Flynn nodded thoughtfully. "Santana's our man."

"But hating them," Bowers said, "doesn't make him sympathetic. I saw something called *ley fuga*. I don't know what it means, but I saw it . . . coming back from Alaejos."

"It's not something new . . . the law of flight. If a prisoner attempts to escape, take the opportunity to shoot him . . . it saves the cost of a trial."

"That's what Santana said."

"He was explaining the practical side."

"I suppose *forcing* the man to escape is practical, too."

"As far as Duro is concerned it is," Flynn said. "But it's happened too often now . . . even right here in Soyopa at Duro's direction. These people have taken a lot from him . . . one injustice after another since the day he arrived. His men are bad, but it's easier to hate one man . . . the one who gives the orders. And now they're going to do something about it."

Bowers looked quickly. "What do you mean?"

"Hilario has figured it out. He says Duro must have known the scalps Lazair gave him were not Apache . . . that time, or times before. He blames Duro more than he does Lazair because Duro is Mexican, even if he is a rurale. I asked him to wait until I'd located you and then we'd talk about it. He has some people at his house; they're ready now to face. Now," Flynn said thoughtfully, "if Santana were to throw his weight against Duro . . ."

"Only that would be mutiny," Bowers said. "If it didn't work, he'd be shot."

"What do you think would happen to Hilario?" Flynn went on. "Put yourself in his place . . . his entire family was massacred, his daughter was forced to live with the men who did the killing. Lazair is out in the hills somewhere, that's something to think about later; but Duro, the one who *bought* the scalps, is here, probably on his bed drunk. Now what would you do?"

"I don't know. I suppose look for some guns."

Flynn half smiled. "They need more than guns. Right now they're up in the air. Hilario's been talking to his friends all morning. Between them they've got a few old pieces that wouldn't shoot across the square; but that doesn't matter now. What happened to Hilario's family does. They'd throw rocks if that's all that was handy. Still, more than guns they need timing, and somebody looking at this who isn't so close to the forest . . ."

It was clear to Bowers the moment they entered Hilario's adobe.

Hilario Esteban with the tightness in his face—sharp-featured now, the look of an old man gone from his eyes—and his hand holding the rusted Burnside .54 muzzle up, the stock resting on the floor. Hilario stood by the window. Five, six other men were there—threadbare white peon clothes and rope-soled shoes, patient faces that were now tired of being patient, but knew no other expression. Three of them were armed with old model rifles, older than Hilario's whose carbine had seen at least twenty years of service; and the remaining three carried knives—long-bladed knives ideal for cutting mesquite branches for cook fires, but knives that could hack through other things equally well. An old woman in black, her head covered, stooping in front of the hearth, stirring atole . . . because even when men made war, even when they were at the end of their patience, they still had to eat. A young girl was next to the old woman. That must be Nita. And as she looked up, hearing them enter the room, Bowers thought: No wonder Flynn went back alone to get her.

La Mosca stood up now in front of the smoke-blackened hearth. She looked at Flynn and said, "During the night I examined Hilario's daughter. There is no sign that she was molested and she is in good health."

Flynn noticed Bowers' quick, surprised glance, and feeling the warm flush over his face he saw the others looking at him also. Why the devil is she telling me that! The curandera, he thought, must be looking into the future again. He nodded to La Mosca and then looked quickly toward Hilario, saying, "I'm glad you haven't done anything yet. Now we can talk it over and do the right thing."

Hilario shook his head. "We waited because you asked us to. But the time for that has passed. We have been waiting a long time for this Duro to become a human being; now we have proof it could never happen to him."

"Duro has a force behind him, well armed," Flynn answered. "That's why I say wait and go about this cautiously."

Hilario nodded to one of the men. "At the home of Ramón's brother, others are waiting, most of them with arms. In the space of minutes we can call dozens more." He shook his head doggedly. "This has been going on too long, Davíd."

Flynn nodded. "All right. But losing more lives is not the way to avenge those already dead."

"Listen," Hilario said. "We have been thinking about this. It isn't something of a rash moment." He went on, carefully, as if to make sure the men present would remember. "Listen. I am going to Duro's house. To his face I'll accuse him of what he's done and ask him to surrender to the people of Soyopa. Now our men will be watching from the square. If he demonstrates in any way, or, if I do not return, then our men will attack the arsenal beneath Duro's quarters. Then we will be ready for Duro's rurales should they object. After this, the first thing will be ridding Soyopa of the men of Lazair." He said this very simply as if it involved merely asking them to leave.

Flynn was about to speak, but Hilario held up his hand

and said, "Now you would ask, 'But what of the government? What will they do?' All right. Porfiristas will come from Mexico City to investigate. What will we tell them? The truth. What Duro is doing is unlawful. Stopping him would be acting in behalf of the government."

Flynn said quietly, "All right. But you're not going to see Duro alone."

"Davíd, this is my problem, as alcalde."

Flynn smiled. "You make things sound more simple than they are. I would say there are other interests involved now." He looked at Nita Esteban who was watching him and their eyes met and held. He had said it naturally, thinking the words only as he said them, as if instinctively, and he thought, smiling within: Maybe La Mosca has cast a spell. Well—

He heard Hilario say, "All right. First we will eat and then we will finish with this."

Hilario leaned the Burnside against the wall and turned nodding to Nita and La Mosca to serve the atole and as he did this they heard the shot. It sounded muffled, far away, from off the square somewhere.

Bowers looked up and at Flynn. "What was that?"

"A pistol."

There was silence in the room. Then, as they moved toward the door there was a flurry of shots—muffled, then louder, echoing through the square and with the gunfire the sound of a running horse.

They were outside now, all of them except the women who stood in the doorway. The sound of horses reached them again a minute later, but none were seen passing the end of the street.

A man rounded the corner from the square and ran toward them. Nearing them, he cried, "It is done! The rurales and the hunters of Indians are at war!"

Hilario said, "Man, speak calmly now and tell what happened."

The man was breathing hard with the excitement of what

he was about to tell and now he inhaled slowly to calm himself, taking his time, because waiting for news makes it the more delicious when it comes.

"The one this man shot," he said, indicating Flynn, "was carried out of the shop by two of his friends, but one remained, the one called War-ren, because he was too drunk to move."

Hilario interrupted, "Who was this you shot?"

"I'll tell you after," Flynn said. And to the man, "Go on."

"The one called War-ren remained, lying with his head on the table, unable to raise it, it seemed." The man smiled as he said, "Now Sergeant Santana was there and he noticed this one. He looked at him for some time and you could see that he was thinking. Some of his rurales were there and he told one of them to bring a riata from his saddle and when he was back with it, they took the one called War-ren, who was still not conscious, to the small closet in the rear of the room, and somehow, with the rope, they secured him upright so that he appeared to be standing up, though his arms and his head hung limp."

The man's smile broadened, saying, "Now Sergeant Santana returned to a table and within a few minutes the two friends of War-ren returned. They couldn't have buried the one who was shot, they returned so soon, but must have thrown his body somewhere. They stood at the bar, unmindful that War-ren was no longer present and now Sergeant Santana approached the one called Loo and he said, 'Listen' —the man attempted to imitate Santana's tone of voice— 'that American was a good shot . . .' meaning you, señor," he said to Flynn. "Then Santana said, 'Are all Americans that capable with firearms?' Now these two Americans winked at one another and the one called Loo said, 'I saw your men shoot that Apache boy in the courtyard. If I could not outshoot any of them I would quit.'

"Now Santana said, 'Listen. You didn't see me shoot the day. I think I am better than the others.' And the one called Loo replied, 'I doubt it, but if you want a little match, let us go outside.' And Santana said, in a tone which was a monument to tranquility, 'Why not have it right here, out of the sun's heat?' To which the American agreed.

"Now Santana boldly walked to the end of the room, bringing a chair and a tumbler with him. He placed the chair with its back rest against the closet door and balanced the tumbler so that it rested on the chair but leaned against the door. Then, walking back to the American he said, 'After you . . .' with the politeness of a gachupín caballero. The American nodded and with that, raised his pistol, aimed and fired."

The man paused, looking around the group. Dramatically, hushed, he said, "The glass shattered."

"That was the first of the shots we heard," Hilario said.

The man scowled at the alcalde, the scowl turning to a smile as he said, "Now listen. Santana turned to the man congratulating him and then said, 'Perhaps we should look in the closet to make sure there is nothing breakable inside of it.' The one called Loo said, 'What difference does it make?' And Santana shrugged saying, 'Merely as a courtesy to the owner of Las Quince Letras.'

"Now we watched closely as they approached the closet. Santana's gun was out of its holster for he was to shoot next. He moved the chair. The one called Loo opened the door and at that moment you should have seen the look on his face! He had holstered his pistol and suddenly he attempted to draw it, but Santana's pistol was pointed directly at this one's stomach and with a coolness that made us shudder, he pulled the trigger once and then again as the man fell.

"The other American was still toward the front at the bar. He drew his pistol and fired, missing, then ran for the door. Santana and his rurales followed him to the door, firing their pistols, but that one reached his horse and escaped.

"Then Santana began gathering bottles of mescal from the bar, telling his companions to do the same, all of the time shouting, 'Now it is done! The time has come! First the gringos and then Duro!' And then he described Duro in the vilest language saying, repeating, his time had come. They rode away then and I saw them stop before the Lieutenant Duro's house, but they remained there only for a moment, taking a horse which the rurale who was on duty there mounted and rode after them down the street toward their camp . . . I assume, now, to gather the others."

The man had finished. Looking at Hilario, Flynn said quietly, "Santana has said it for us. The time has come—"

Seventeen

●

Curt Lazair reined in, holding his mount within the shadow of Santo Tomás' east wall, and from there watched the rurale patrol swing into the square, seeing most of the horsemen riding out again by way of the street that led to their camp. He saw Bowers then, dismounting with those who had remained, in front of Las Quince Letras.

Flies buzzed at the canvas bag that hung from Lazair's saddle horn. He waved his hand at them idly and, still watching the men in front of the mescal shop, he sniffed as the rancid odor of the scalps rose from the bag. He did this instinctively, as an animal sniffs the air, still, he was not fully aware that he had done so. There was a question in his mind and the answer to it could be a hell of a lot more dangerous than the smell of day-old scalps. And now, suddenly, he thought he was looking at the answer—

A rurale patrol . . . been out in the hills . . . that shavetail with them . . . he knew where the camp was, because he'd been there. That must be it!

Lazair had been thinking about it all the way in . . . calmly at first, because that was the best way to go about things like this; go over it slow and everything will fall into place . . . then he had found Sid's body—not all of it because the buzzards had found Sid first—and the calm thinking ended then and there.

Two dead, one wounded. And not even the wounded man —who was shot clean through a lung and wouldn't last another day—or the man who had brought him in, the only one of the four who was still healthy, had seen who had done the shooting. That didn't happen every day: three men shot up and not even knowing who did it.

But now it was plain to Lazair. Bowers and the rurale patrol . . . it couldn't be anyone else!

He crossed the square along the east side, following the adobe fronts around to Duro's house. The rurale guard sat leaning against the door to the arsenal. He was asleep and did not look up even as Lazair rode up close to him and dismounted.

Lamas Duro jumped with the abrupt sound of the door opening. Sitting behind the desk he stiffened, looking up with startled wide-eyed surprise, and a roll of silver coins spilled from his fingers to the desk top. The coins scattered, rolling into silver pesos already stacked in neat columns on the desk, ten coins to a column, 100 pesos in each.

Lazair stood in the doorway, confidently, defiantly, the way a man stands who has two Colts strapped to his thighs. One hand rested idly on the handle of the right pistol; the fingers of the other hand were curled in the drawstring of the canvas sack. His eyes held on Duro, coming to conclusions then and there, seeing the money, the look on Duro's face, the way he was dressed—ready to travel—jacket, scarf, gun belt and the Chihuahua hat at one end of the desk.

"Where're you going?"

It was still on Duro's face, the shock of seeing Lazair suddenly in front of him, but now he tried to smile. "It's time for a patrol."

"Your sergeant just come off one."

"This is a different kind." Duro smiled. "I am going to

ride out alone. Perhaps one man can find out more than twenty."

"About what?"

"Apaches."

Lazair was silent, his eyes remaining on Duro. Suddenly, "You've had enough, so now you think it's time to haul out."

"What are you talking about?"

"You should have waited for a report before you started counting your money."

"I was just putting aside the amount owed to you from the last time," Duro explained.

"Not when you never expected to see me again you weren't." Lazair moved toward the desk, his hand still on the pistol butt. "That boy-cavalry-soldier told you where we lived . . . so you got it in your head: Hit 'em . . . sometime after it's dark and it will save passing out *muchos pesos.*" Lazair said again, "You should have made sure before counting your money."

"That makes no sense," Duro said slowly and now the question furrowing his forehead was genuine. "Who hit your camp?"

Lazair smiled faintly. "You're getting better." He said then, "Your sergeant'll be coming in pretty soon . . . he's over to the cantina now. When he gets enough brave juice in him he'll come and tell you how they got only two for sure 'cause somebody couldn't hold his nerves and started shooting before they found out hardly nobody was home."

"I don't follow you," Duro said, still frowning. "Got two of what?"

"Two of my boys!"

Duro's features relaxed with amazement. "No!" and then the smile began forming slowly, curling the corners of his mouth. "Santana did that!" The smile widening, "I can't believe it. He wouldn't have the nerve."

"He got it somewhere," Lazair said. "My men followed and he ambushed them."

Duro shook his head slowly, considering this. "No . . . it could not have been Santana."

"You know goddamn well it was!"

"I swear I know nothing of this!"

"Who else is there?"

"Apaches."

"They'd a been messier."

Duro was silent, his eyes roaming the room slowly, but picturing other things. He said suddenly, bringing his palm down slapping the desk, "The other American! He's not been here for two days!"

"One man couldn't have raised all that hell."

"Maybe we don't know him," Duro said thoughtfully.

Lazair half smiled. "But I know you . . . and I've got eyes . . . counting your money . . . all dressed up for a trip. . . ."

"Listen . . . I swear on the grave of my mother I know nothing of this! I am counting this now to pay you what is owed . . . putting it aside to have it ready for you . . . you come at odd times, so I considered: The next time he comes it will be ready—" Duro hesitated and smiled at Lazair confidently. "Look . . . this is silly what you've been thinking. Let's have a drink now, together, and then I'll finish counting this."

He nodded to the sack in Lazair's hand. "You have more. Good. I'll pay you for those too; and then the account will be up to date. How many do you have there? No—wait until after we have a drink. This is a feast day, we should have a drink together." He looked suddenly in the direction of the square then back to Lazair. "Was that a shot?"

Lazair did not move. "That one was off somewhere. It's the one that rings in your ear for half a second that you worry about. Then it's all over." He said it with his hand on the gun butt and the meaning was clear.

"Everyone talks of death today," Duro said, and made himself laugh. "But look, even with the talking of death there is an equal amount of drinking." He said then, winking, "You know you can frighten the devil only so long. When there is no more mescal he comes and inserts a demon in your head. Now the demon hates this confinement and he runs from one side to the other butting at the sensitive walls of one's head." He raised a hand to his forehead and the fingers spread over the shape of it delicately. "Señor," he said, smiling through a frown which was meant to indicate a headache, "would you kindly consent to a glass of something?"

Lazair did not smile. He looked at Duro silently and his contempt for the rurale lieutenant was in his eyes, in the features that did not move, and grimly evident in the hard line of his mouth. "Get your drink," he said curtly. Duro started from the desk and Lazair added, "I'm right behind you."

He stood in the doorway to the sleeping room and watched Duro take a fresh bottle of mescal from the cupboard next to the bed, then stepped aside as Duro passed him, going to the desk again. Duro sat down and as he opened the desk drawer, Lazair said, "If you're smart you'll just come out with glasses."

Duro looked up. "Of course."

They drank in silence, Duro filling the glasses quickly as they were emptied; Lazair watching him, in no hurry, wondering what Duro would do, willing to take all the time necessary to find out.

Duro looked up suddenly. "Did you hear it? Another one!"

Lazair was half sitting with his left hip on the edge of the desk, resting the mescal glass on his thigh. He looked down at Duro calmly. "You hear all kinds of noises during a fiesta."

But with the sudden bursts of gunfire that followed, Lazair came off the desk. He moved to the door quickly, still holding his drink, still half watching Duro, and as the rurale lieutenant started to rise, Lazair snapped, "Stay where you are!"

He opened the door and the sound of a running horse

rose from the square. He saw the rider, one of his men, reaching a side street and the rurales in front of the cantina firing after him.

The glass flew out of Lazair's hand shattering against the desk and in that instant a pistol was in his right hand pointed at Duro. "You didn't know!"

He wanted to pull the trigger. It rushed to his mind, but a judgment was already there; it had prevented him from killing Duro before and now it was there again with its cold reason making him slow down, making him grip the pistol tighter. If he killed Duro he would be through. Not just in this part of Sonora, but everywhere in Mexico. He'd have to go back to the States, where he was wanted, and spend the rest of his life on the dodge. He'd have to take his chances in the States because if he were caught he'd be better off than if he were pulled in by the Mexican authorities. That's what stopped him. Don't throw away a good thing: a safe place to live and a profitable business just because of one man. But it occurred to Lazair then, at that moment, that Duro was through. The only thing was, this wasn't the time or the place.

More calmly he said to Duro, "You didn't know, eh . . . ?"

"I swear to Almighty God I didn't! What happened out there?" Duro was rising again.

"Stay put!" Lazair snapped. He looked at Duro and then out again. He kept his eyes on the front of the mescal shop and when Santana and two rurales came out, shouting, mounting their horses, Lazair pulled the door quickly, almost closed, and watched them through an inch opening. They came toward the house, shouting something. When they were directly below, Lazair could not see them, but he heard Duro's name and suddenly they were riding away— four of them now, the last one, the rurale who had been on guard, on Lazair's mount.

Lazair looked at Duro and his gaze held steadily. "Something's going on. Santana and the two with him had a jug of mescal in each hand. They stopped here then rode off toward the rurale camp."

"They always drink after a patrol," Duro said.

"They were hollering something about you."

"What?"

"I couldn't make it out."

"Perhaps calling out to me."

"Does he do that often?"

Duro hesitated. "No . . ."

"Something's going on," Lazair said again. He waited, watching the square, feeling a tension that he could not understand. After a few minutes it occurred to him to run over to the mescal shop to see what had happened, then keep going to camp and move it someplace else before doing anything. There would be time enough to pay back Duro.

Looking out over the square he saw them as soon as they appeared from the side street and started across the openness. He was not sure how many there were at first, because they seemed to be all wearing peon clothes with so much white blending together, from this distance a crowd of white cotton cloth with darker spots that were faces and straw sombreros. Then he realized there were not as many as he thought. Perhaps ten altogether. And—the two cavalrymen! He squinted, watching them come closer, making sure, and when he was certain they were coming here he glanced at Duro.

"Come here . . . you've got company."

Duro rose, hesitantly now. "Who? I don't hear anyone."

"You will."

"Who is it?"

"See for yourself."

Lazair opened the door, taking Duro's arm, and pushed him suddenly out to the veranda. He closed the door again, seeing Duro, seeing Duro's eyes as he turned. Lazair pushed his pistol threateningly through the door opening and Duro turned back toward the square.

Hilario pointed with the Burnside. "There he is."

Bowers said curiously, "Was that someone behind him?"

"It looked like it," Flynn said. He looked up, watching Duro, noticing the man's hesitancy, his reluctance to stand at the rail and look down at them.

"He seems afraid," Hilario whispered.

"He should be," Flynn said. "If he heard Santana."

Watching Duro, Hilario said, "If I were to raise this barrel two inches, and pull the trigger, it would be accomplished."

Flynn said, "You know better than that."

"I wish I did not," Hilario answered. And now he called out, "Señor Duro, we would speak with you."

They heard Duro's voice faintly. "Come back another time."

"This will not keep," Hilario called. "Already too much time has passed."

Duro hesitated. Then rested his hands firmly on the railing and looking down now he seemed suddenly more sure of himself, as if the mescal he had drunk was now making his head lighter, his senses keener. He said, "Listen, alcalde, when I want to speak to you, I'll send rurales. You'll come at that time and at no other. Now go home . . . and take your friends with you." He started to turn.

"Duro!" Flynn called the name sharply and the rurale lieutenant turned back again. "We'd like to speak to you."

Duro looked down at them coldly. To Flynn he said, "I have invited you before to come to my house, thinking you would come as a gentleman . . . but when you accompany animals, then perhaps you should be treated as one."

Flynn could feel the sudden heat on his face, but he restrained the impulse to raise his voice and he said mildly, "What happened to your manners?"

"There's no need for them since you are neglecting to use your own."

Flynn smiled to himself. Now it comes out: the real Duro. But why the change of face all of a sudden? Maybe Santana scared him into reality. He's so busy thinking what he's going to do next, there's no time for the polite front. He heard

Bowers saying, in a low voice, "He doesn't want us to come up there."

Flynn called up, "Hilario Esteban has something to say. He'll do all the talking."

"Then why are you here," Duro returned, "if this doesn't concern you? And if I choose not to speak to him at this time, that doesn't concern you either." Flynn felt his patience ebbing; but he would try it once more. He began, "Lieutenant . . ." but that was all—

The gunfire came suddenly, a scattering of rifle shots off beyond Duro's house. Flynn looked at the others; they were standing still, wondering; then some were moving hurriedly to the head of the street that led to the rurale camp. Now, from the other direction, came faintly screams and shouts and a few people were reaching the square coming from the streets on both sides of the church, some of the people who had been celebrating the fiesta at the cemetery. They were calling something. The sound of horses now from the street siding Duro's house and a half-dozen rurales were galloping into the square. Their cries were shrill, unintelligible with the sharp clatter of the hoofs . . . then one word was clear . . . and it was a shriek that hung hot in the air like a knife blade raised in the sunlight—

"APACHES!"

Eighteen

●

It is always the same when you hear it . . . a feeling you can't describe . . . and right away you are picturing them, even if you've never seen one, and nine times out of ten the cry comes after they've gone—*Apaches!* . . . A dust cloud in the distance if you're quick, if you get there soon after; but usually the sign is cold and the man lying there, the survivor, cannot tell you which way they went . . . not with the sun scalding fire-red inside of his head because the Apaches have taken his eyelids . . . and other parts of him. First patrol . . . and the heavy flat sound of the sergeant's revolving pistol finishing off the buck who had been shot through the legs.

Apaches! Again and again and again . . . and the instantaneous tight throb that the word brings never changes because it is not something a man gets used to. But the reaction that comes a split second later, that changes. In a short time it changes from natural panic to trying to remember everything you know about the Apache in a few seconds; and after a half dozen years of it, when it's your business, your reaction instantly eliminates what will not help you here and now and you think of the Apache as pertaining only to this particular place, this particular time.

And that's what Flynn was doing—picturing the south side of Soyopa, where the rurale camp was, where the firing was coming from—it was open country for miles, stretching, curving east and west. So the main threat was not here, even though the firing was coming from that direction now. No, the north side, beyond the cemetery, there it was close with brush, uneven country.

And now, running to the head of the street where most of the others were, Flynn glanced across the square and saw more people coming hurriedly along both sides of the church.

Now it's Soldado's turn—it went through Flynn's mind. Something has stirred him up good.

Past the end of the street, beyond a rise a good two hundred yards off, the bleached tops of the tents were visible. There was smoke and scattered gunfire and suddenly, coming up the rise, up into the street, were the rurales, Santana with them, and as they rode into the square Santana was shouting for them to fan out in a circle, on all sides of the pueblo.

"Sergeant Santana!" Hilario ran close in front of the sergeant's horse as he reined in. "What is it?"

"The Anti-Christ! What do you think!"

"But how did they come?"

"Suddenly . . . as they always do!"

"Did you lose men?"

"Several," Santana answered, swinging down, breathing hard, watching his men disappear down the streets on all sides of the square. "They struck suddenly, riding almost directly through our camp; then they were gone, leaving some of the tents afire, moving out, away, but seeming to circle to the other side of the pueblo."

Flynn said, "You're going after them?"

"After them! Soldado Viejo is here in force. He would like us to come out after him . . . so he can cut us to pieces. He is here with men! Something has happened to his thinking. Before he would raid perhaps smaller pueblos, but most of the times herders and then with never more than two dozen men. Now he has over a hundred!"

"See that your men are circling the entire village," Hilario told him, looking about anxiously.

"I know my job!"

Bowers was looking across the square toward the church where more people were entering the square. "You hear them? They're yelling Apache. God, they must be close . . ."

"That's the side," Flynn said. "They can come up close because of the brush . . . that's where most of them will be. The strike at the rurale camp was to finish them off quick, but it didn't work."

Hilario's head turned about, wide-eyed. "We should go over there, then."

"What about Duro?" Flynn asked, turning, looking up at him. The lieutenant stood holding tight to the railing, looking, staring across the square.

"Ah, Señor Duro," Hilario said. "I remember his own words once . . . let me see . . ." And then he called out, "Duro!" The lieutenant's gaze dropped down to Hilario, surprised, as if he had forgotten they were there. "Duro! Stay in your house until we return. There will be a man here. If he sees your head come out of the door, he will shoot it!"

As they passed the church, many of the people were crowding into its wide doorway which the Franciscan padre stood holding open. Flynn saw him wave to them as they passed and then they were hurrying down the side wall shadow of the church and beyond, deserted now, they could see the cemetery—the rows of wooden crosses and mounds of stones and scattered here and there the remains of the fiesta which would not be finished today: mescal bottles, ollas, plates of pottery and on three or four of the crosses hung sombreros. These moved. As the faint breeze came down from the hills it stirred the wide hat brims, turning them lazily, and this was the only movement now in the deserted cemetery.

Beyond, scattered mesquite thickets began their creeping in from the wild country and beyond the brush were piñon and scrub oak, then jackpine as the ground rose to deep-green and brown-green hills and over all of this nothing moved.

He's smart, Flynn thought, thinking of Soldado. If a white man had the upper hand he'd stand out there showing himself, defying you to come out. Soldado's smart. He makes you think he's gone, and when you go out . . . then he has you.

They stood in the backyard of the adobe which was across the road from the church, looking out over a low wall. Bowers' eyes were half closed as his head swung slowly, squinting into the brush shadows, seeing nothing. "They're gone," he said finally.

Hilario shook his head, disagreeing. "Why should they go?"

Bowers said, "Dave, what do you think?"

"I think Hilario answered it," Flynn replied. "Why should they go?"

"You don't see them!"

"When did you ever?" Flynn spoke quietly, staring out at the thickets. "Something has aroused Soldado . . ." He hesitated. "Maybe Lazair stumbled onto his rancheria while the men were away . . . whatever the reason, it must be a good one to make him throw his men at an entire village. He attacked when he was hot, and it wasn't successful, but now he's cooled off. Whatever he came for, he must still want, because he didn't get anything. There's no one here who's going to go out after him, so there's no reason for him to leave. He has all the time in the world . . . good cover . . . and he's Apache. Now you tell me what he'll do."

Bowers said, after a silence, "And what are we going to do?"

"Wait."

"For how long?"

"That's up to Soldado," Flynn said. "Probably nothing will

happen tonight, but in the morning something might." Bowers looked at him curiously and he added, "That rider of Lazair's that Santana chased out of town . . . he's on his way to their camp now, if Soldado didn't spot him. By morning he should be rushing back here with the rest of them, yelling for rurales, but they'll find Apaches instead."

Bowers' face brightened. "Then that's our chance!"

Flynn shook his head. "Soldado will know about them before they know about him."

They separated soon after this, stringing out in the backyards of the adobes, watching the brush and the trees and the shadows that crept toward them as the sun began to fade. Then there were the evening sounds which seemed quieter than day sounds, and the smell of wood fires. Mesquite burning. Bowers was in the next yard, a hundred feet from Flynn, Hilario was beyond him, in his own yard. And now it was getting dark quickly.

There was Nita, coming out of the back door, moving across the yard toward her father. She was carrying something and Flynn thought: Probably atole. We eat and Soldado eats, but that's all we have in common with him. He watched Nita go to Bowers next and as she came closer he could see her face more clearly. Then she was approaching him with the atole—the flour gruel—carrying it in a tin pot, her other hand carrying pottery bowls, and he felt an excitement inside of him. And telling himself it was silly, repeating it quickly as she drew closer, did not make it go away.

"Are you hungry?"

He shook his head. "No. But it would be best to eat something."

"There was not time to prepare anything better than this." She kept her eyes down most of the time, but when she did look at Flynn, when their eyes met, they would hold and there was no other living soul on the earth.

"I don't mind atole, I've had it many times before."

He said, unexpectedly then, "If it were darker, I think I would kiss you."

Her eyes rose to his. "If it were darker, I think I would let you." They looked at each other in silence, then she rose and moved toward the next yard with the pot of atole.

Later, after it had been dark almost an hour, a man came to him. It was Ramón who had been in Hilario's house with the others.

"We think they are approaching."

"Where?"

"Directly out from my yard"—he waved his arm in the darkness—"which is the other side of Hilario's. Before it was dark we saw this Apache who seemed to be showing himself purposely, making strange signs, as if tempting us to come out. Then for a while he was gone. Then, after the darkness came, we heard faint sounds. They have stopped now, but you'd better come."

Hilario and Bowers were there, crouched behind the low stone wall.

Ramón asked in a whisper that was nervously harsh, "Has anything occurred?"

Bowers nodded to them. Hilario looked up and said quickly, "He is close now, but out of sight. A moment ago there was a sound, it seemed a hiss, but I'm sure it was a word."

Flynn said, *"Si-kisn?"*

"Yes, that was it!" Hilario whispered excitedly.

"He was telling you," Flynn said, "that he's a brother, a friend."

"It is a ruse," Hilario whispered.

"Perhaps," Flynn said. "But when an Apache fights at night, it is because he has no other choice. Soldado has time. He has more of it than we have."

Bowers said, "And maybe he's planning on your thinking that way."

He's learning fast, Flynn thought, and said, "You never know them so well you don't have to take chances." He knelt close to the wall now and cupping his hands to his mouth he called in a low, drawn-out hiss, *"Si-kisnnnn."*

There was dead silence. Then the word came back from not far away. Again silence, and suddenly the dim shape of an Apache was standing across the wall from them. He said, "Flín?"

Flynn rose, and hesitated so there would be no surprise in his voice that would make him speak out loud. Then he said, "Three-cents." He glanced at Bowers and at Hilario. "This is Three-cents, Joe Madora's head Coyotero tracker."

Bowers said, "What!" and clamped his mouth shut because the word was sharp in the stillness.

"Come over," Flynn said to the Coyotero.

"There is another with me," Three-cents said in Spanish, and almost as he said it, he was gone.

"I thought they made army trackers wash," Bowers whispered. "He's filthy."

"The dirt's on purpose," Flynn said. "He wiped saliva on his body and then sand on top of that. That's why we didn't see him."

A moment later, Three-cents was back and behind him another figure was coming, crouched low. Then he rose, and as he spoke, even before he spoke, Flynn was smiling.

The words came as a hoarse whisper—"David, you son of a bitch, I've got to pull you out of another one."

"Joe!" Flynn whispered, and grabbed the man's arm to help him over the wall.

"Let go! You'll rip open the hole!"

"How is it?"

"I'm standing in front of you."

"I never expected to see you again, Joe."

"That's why I can't figure they sent a shortsighted bastard like you on this trip." Madora looked at Bowers then. "How you doin', Red?"

Self-consciously, Bowers said, "All right."

Madora turned from him abruptly. "David, I'm hungrier 'n a bastard. What've you got?"

Hilario said, "Nita will bring something."

But Flynn said, "We'll go in and get it. Joe, you and your boy come along and I'll fix you up."

When they were near the house, Madora said, "Those boys were dyin' for news. They won't take kindly to you rushin' me away."

Flynn ignored this, saying quickly, "Where's Deneen?"

"He's out there."

Flynn relaxed somewhat. "I had a hunch he was. With how many?"

"Counting Coyoteros?"

Flynn nodded. "Yes."

"Ten."

"Ten! How many are scouts?"

"Ten."

"No . . ." Flynn groaned, but there was a humor to this and it struck Flynn and he could not help but smile now. "All right. What happened?"

"About the time Deneen got back to Whipple from his tour, the genral'd found out what he'd done." They had entered the adobe and now, close to the firelight, Madora was smiling. "That was something. The genral dressed hell out of him and the first thing you know Deneen's got a Mexico assignment of his own."

"How'd you find out?"

"Hell, it's all over. Some of it was overheard firsthand . . . a friend of mine. Anyway, your pal was relieved of his adjutant's job and the genral kicks his tail down to Sonora to find a Lieutenant Duro of the rurales . . . cuz the genral says, All right, goddamn it, if we're going to do it, then we're going to do it right. Get your ass down to Mexico and get some permission and if you don't get it, don't come back." Madora added, "Now some say genrals don't talk like that, but my friend says it's gospel."

"But why only ten men?"

"We ain't a war party. The genral told him no soldiers, else it'd be considered invasion of a foreign country, but he said you can take all the trackers you want cuz for cry-sake there's enough goddamn Apaches down there now that nobody's going to notice a few goddamn more."

"I never heard the general talk like that."

"What's that, atole? That's the only thing that's almost not better than nothing."

"Where's Deneen now?"

"About a mile off."

"Apaches spot you?"

"Hell no."

"I'd better go talk to him."

"Somebody better. He like to wet his pants when Three-cents come in and told about Soldado." Madora looked at Flynn quickly, seriously. "This is the first time I've seen him in a tight spot. He can't take it, can he?"

"Why ask me?" Flynn said.

"Because you were in the war with him where there were lots of tight spots." Madora paused and half smiled. "That's what's between you two. You caught him in a jackpot cryin' for his mama."

"You don't get to be colonel that way."

"That's what everybody thinks."

"But that isn't what's bothering us here and now."

"You want to see Deneen. All right, I'll take you to him."

"Maybe he'll come in," Flynn suggested. "It would be safer for him here."

"He won't move."

"All right, then we'll go out."

"In one minute." Madora took heaping spoons of the atole, scraping the plate clean. Three-cents had been eating as they spoke and now they went outside, back to the low wall. Bowers was alone.

"Where's Hilario?" Flynn asked.

"He went to relieve the man watching Duro's house. Dave, what is it?"

"Deneen is here, but with only a few trackers. He was on

his way to talk to Duro about a border campaign when they ran into the Apaches."

"He's fighting them?"

"No, holed up. I'm going out and talk to him. When I get back I'll tell you all about it."

"What if you don't get through?"

Flynn smiled. "If this old man can do it, anybody can."

Madora said mildly, "David, when they passed out proper respect you must've been scratchin' your butt with both hands."

Bowers watched them go over the wall and fade into the darkness. He asked himself: Could you do that? Sure, if you've been doing it as long as they have. What about the first couple of times? He was squinting into the darkness, expecting a sound. You either get used to it, or you don't get used to it. That's the way to look at things like that. He knew this was easy to say and he told himself: Who said anything about getting used to it being easy!

He had thought before that this was not an assignment for a soldier, but now he knew conclusively that he had been wrong. And thinking of soldiers, oddly, he thought of Santana and how Santana considered himself one and boasted that if ever his rurales got the Apaches in open country, then he'd see some soldiering; that's what Santana had intimated.

After this he thought of many things, faraway things, but slowly his thoughts came back to the present. Now . . . and then the morning, a few hours away. What would happen then? Flynn said Lazair's men might come back in the morning, he thought.

That's how it started in his mind, the plan. Just from remembering something Flynn had said, and in the next few minutes the plan began to develop, began to grow into something that might work.

A man crouched next to him in the darkness, startling him.

"What passes?" the man said. "Hilario Esteban relieved me and told me to come here."

Bowers nodded, "It is still quiet," and then quickly, unexpectedly, he asked, "Have you seen the rurale, Santana?"

Nineteen

●

The alcalde, Hilario Esteban, stood beneath the veranda of Lamas Duro's house, and with the Burnside .54 cradled in his arm he looked out over the dark stillness of the square. Far across loomed the dim outline of Santo Tomás and creeping in a wide circle toward him on the two sides were the low, shadowed adobe fronts of the buildings that faced the square. There were no horses in front of Las Quince Letras.

This is the first time in six months that the cantina has been empty, Hilario thought. The time before was the day everyone remained in their houses. The day the rurales came.

But it was just the one day that there was no business, his thoughts continued, for the rurales were inside the cantina as soon as their camp was erected. And soon after, within three days, the people were beginning to go there again; quietly at first, once in a while, then soon with the same frequency as before . . . having adjusted themselves to our new neighbors.

A man can adjust himself to anything.

Still, there is a limit. He thought, now we have reached the limit. We could go on pretending that Lamas Duro is not here, but in doing so we would also be pretending that such a thing as honor still remained. If a man must make excuses for himself, continually argue with himself that he is a man, then he is better off dead. And then he thought: Why do I think about this one man when our worst enemy now surrounds the village? He shook his head faintly. No, Lamas Duro is more the Anti-Christ than Soldado Viejo. He whispered, half aloud, "Saint Francis, help us."

Now and then his eyes would go up the stairways that came down from both ends of the veranda above him, angling toward the center where he stood.

He would look up as the sound came from the room: walking, a squeaking board, and sometimes he thought he heard talking; but he told himself, if so Lamas Duro was talking to himself to keep his spirits up.

And finally it occurred to Hilario: Why not talk to him now? Waiting until Soldado left would be reasonable if you were occupied elsewhere, but here you stand. Go up and talk to him . . . no, tell him . . . and get it over with.

He started up the stairs on the left. Halfway up he stopped, holding himself still. The door above had opened. Slowly, with a long, low squeak. He heard footsteps on the veranda now. Three steps, then silence. Now three more, moving to the other side of the veranda.

Hilario turned slowly, crouching, and eased down until he was sitting on the steps. He raised the Burnside carefully and pointed it toward the opposite stairway. Cocking it will make a noise, he thought, hearing and feeling his heart beating through his body. So don't cock it until you are ready to fire . . . if firing is necessary. But, Saint Francis, don't make it necessary. Make Señor Duro go back inside.

He heard the footsteps again, at the top of the stairs now. Then they were coming down. Hilario held himself tense, squinting in the darkness, and now he could see the dim outline of a man. He waited, holding his breath, watching the figure reach the bottom. Then another sound, above . . . another man was on the stairs!

Two of them . . . how can that be!

His eyes fought the darkness, studying the second dim shape almost at the bottom of the stairs now. That one is Duro! I know it is!

Hilario Esteban rose suddenly, bringing up the Burnside, pulling back the hammer. "Señor Duro—stand where you are!"

And with the suddenness of this the first man was running. Hilario ignored him. Duro stood at the bottom of the stairs looking across and up at him.

"Who is it!"

"Hilario Esteban!"

He could hear the sound of the other man on the hard-packed square and suddenly the shadowy form of Duro was not in front of him, but running, sprinting into the open darkness of the square.

"Señor Duro!"

Quick, rapid-sharp boot steps in the openness . . .

"Señor Duro! Halt!"

A dim form growing dimmer . . . fifty, sixty, seventy feet . . .

The Burnside came up, cheek level. "Señor Duro! . . ."

Eighty . . .

"Saint Francis help me!" And with it the heavy dull explosion of the Burnside.

Lamas Duro took six more strides, though he was not conscious of them . . . for he was dead the instant the heavy ball slammed into his back.

"Here he comes," Madora said.

"He's half animal," Flynn whispered, belly-down next to Madora in a shallow gully, watching the dim form creeping noiselessly toward them through the brush.

"He's all animal," Madora grunted and rolled to his side to face Three-cents as the Coyotero dropped into the gully with them. They were returning the same way Madora and the Coyotero had come—Three-cents going ahead to see that the way was clear, then either signaling them on or crawling back to get them if he considered an audible ani-mal-sound signal dangerous. This way, if they ran into Soldado's Apaches, Three-cents would meet them first, and there was the chance they would think him one of their own. Even recognizing him as not a Mimbreño would take time and Three-cents would have his chance to act.

In his own language, but with a word here and there of Spanish, he informed them that Mimbres were just ahead.

"There are three," he told them. "They stand listening. Then two will move in opposite directions, but always one remains in the same place."

"Like army pickets," Flynn whispered.

Madora muttered, "They've been doing it for five hundred years." They were silent then, thinking, but finally Madora said, "Well, let's go take him."

"Who's doing the honors?"

"Whoever sees him first."

They crawled out of the gully one at a time, Three-cents leading, and kept to the brush patches as they went over the flat ground. Just ahead now they could make out the dense blackness of trees, a soft crooked line against the night sky, and when Three-cents glanced back at them they knew that there the Mimbre waited.

They moved up on both sides of the Coyotero and he said, with his mouth close to the ground, "Thirty paces into the trees he stands. The two come out to the edge before going opposite ways." They were silent again, watching, and then Three-cents muttered, "There," pushing his arm out in front of him on the ground.

It was visible for a moment, like an off-white speck of shadow and then gone.

"He's sure of himself," Madora grunted, "wearing a white breechclout at night." They waited several minutes, giving the two Mimbre vedettes time to move off, out of hearing; then they crawled toward the trees.

Pines. The scent was heavy. Flynn could feel the needles in the sand beneath his hands and knees, and now a branch brushed his face. He had not brought the Springfield. It would be in the way. But he could feel his pistol under his left arm and a clasp knife was in his pocket.

Watch Three-cents now, Flynn thought. He'll call it. They waited for the Mimbre to move, to cause a sound that would tell where he was, but no sound came and as the minutes passed they knew they would have to bring the Mimbre to them.

Three-cents rose silently and moved off from them a dozen steps before sinking down, huddling close among pine branches. A low moan came from him then, in the stillness a long low gasp of pain.

Flynn waited. Come on. That's one of your brothers in trouble. Come on and find him. Still there was no sound, but at that moment he felt the movement; he sensed it and from the corner of his eye there he was, the Mimbre, crouched low, moving toward Three-cents. Wait. Nothing sudden. Let him get past you. Joe's seen him too. Joe probably smelled him.

The Mimbre stopped. In the moaning tone, a word in the Mimbreño dialect came from Three-cents. And in the corner of Flynn's eye the Mimbre moved again. All right, get him.

But as he rose, Madora was suddenly, silently behind the Mimbre and the next moment his arms were around him, forearm viselike against the throat and hand clamped over the mouth, dragging the warrior to the ground with him. Three-cents stood over them. Without hesitating he pushed his knife into the Mimbre's chest.

They went on, carrying the Apache, for he could not be left there for the others to find. When it's light, Flynn thought, they'll read the signs. That will make it harder to get back. But what might happen after sunup was something to think of then. They moved on through the darkness.

Three-cents signaled when they neared the place where the others were. A soft low whistle . . . silence . . . then an answering whistle and within a minute there were Coyotero scouts all around them.

"Where is he?" Flynn said to Madora. Here was another pine stand and in the darkness he could see only the Coyoteros standing close by.

Madora pointed. "He was right over there before."

"You'd think three men walking in at night would interest him."

"He's got enough troubles without looking for more."

"Joe, there's another problem now we didn't count on before." He indicated the dead Mimbre. "Tonight they'll miss him; tomorrow they'll be getting in each other's way looking for him."

Madora nodded. "I agree."

"So," Flynn went on, "if we're going back to the village, it's got to be tonight or not at all."

"But," Madora said, "you got to convince Deneen crawling through their line's the thing to do—anytime."

"I'll convince him," Flynn said, and looked at the Mimbre again. "We'd better get rid of him."

"We'll bury him."

"When we go back it should be in two or three groups. What do you think?"

Madora nodded. "I'll work it out with Three-cents, you go talk to Horse's-ass."

Colonel Deneen was lying down, head on his saddle bag and a blanket covering him as Flynn entered the small clearing Deneen had reserved for himself; but in one abrupt movement the blanket was thrown back and he was sitting up, pointing a pistol at Flynn.

"Who is it?"

"Flynn." He started to explain, "Madora brought me out . . ." but he stopped. God, he should know that much.

"Well, goddamn it, sit down! I don't care for you standing there looming over me!"

"I didn't mean to frighten you."

"You didn't frighten me, I assure you. Where's Bowers?"

"Soyopa."

"Why didn't he come?"

"It wasn't necessary."

Sitting down, Flynn studied the man, trying to see the face clearly in the darkness. The face had changed, but he could not make out details other than it being in need of a shave, perhaps drawn. Bluntly now, Flynn asked, "What are you going to do?"

"I haven't decided."

"It's less than four hours to daylight."

"So?"

"We killed a Mimbre on the way out. As soon as it's light they'll be looking for him."

"So?"

"So we'll have to start back to the village now while it's still dark," Flynn said patiently.

"And since I happen to command, and don't choose to go to the village, what then?"

"It would be better if you went."

"Are you threatening me, Flynn?"

God, he's sitting on the edge of his nerves! "Of course I'm not threatening. I'm reminding you that with the sun something's bound to happen. It would be too late then to get back to the village and those people might need all the help they can get."

Abruptly then, in a tone intended to sound calm, natural, Deneen said, "I suppose you were surprised to find me here."

Flynn nodded. "Somewhat."

"The general decided I had better look into this myself, since it has possibilities of an extensive border campaign. It's been my argument right along, one push from both sides of the border will squeeze every Apache man, woman and child out of the hills right where we want them." As he said this, his voice sounded natural.

He's been rehearsing this one, Flynn thought.

Deneen went on, "I'm contacting the local rurale officer first . . . at my own time. Do you know him?"

Flynn nodded.

"There in that village?"

Flynn nodded again.

"Well goddamn it speak up! What's his authority!"

"Do you really want to know?"

"What!"

Flynn's voice was calm. "Look, there are only a few hours until light. I think it would be wise if we started back right now instead of sitting here playing games. I know why you're here. Everyone does, and you know it. And I'll tell you this . . . I don't give a good damn what happened between you and the general. That's past history, to me it's as dead as what happened that night at Chancellorsville. You've made that one live on even when I was trying to forget it, and now you throw this border campaign nonsense in my face and expect me to swallow it, pretending you're on a secret mission . . . like I've been doing with Bowers for the past week —trying to act like this is an honest-to-God assignment; half wanting to help him keep his faith in the army, half wanting to tell him what a real son of a bitch you really are, but not having the heart because to him a colonel, even you, is a rank that takes time, guts and a military mind." Flynn stopped, but abruptly he added, "Why did you send him?"

Deneen stared with the rage plain in his face, even in the darkness, and he was not able to speak.

"Maybe I can answer it myself," Flynn said, watching Deneen closely. He started out slowly, "Bowers' father, the brigadier, was there. Maybe he saw you do it . . . or he was in the medical tent after and could tell gunshot from shrapnel and had time to figure where a doctor there wouldn't. Either way, you were aware of his knowing. Perhaps you'd forgotten it over the years, but when the boy showed up at Whipple there it was again and you took it for granted the brigadier had told his boy about the cowardly act of a Captain Deneen one night at Chancellorsville. If Bowers knows about it, he's not saying, but the chances are remote that he even does, because his father wasn't the kind of man to let it get beyond him. But maybe he should have told . . . and had you drummed out of the service. No, you should have resigned yourself. But instead you stuck it out, because after the war there wouldn't be any more Chancellorsvilles . . . and now some men have paid with their lives because you're a rotten officer and not honest enough to admit it . . . because two men you think know about a mistake you once made, you conclude the only thing to do is get rid of them before *everybody* knows." Flynn paused. "Your big mistake was pointing that pistol at your foot—you were about five feet too low."

"Is that all you have to say, Flynn?" Deneen kept his voice calm.

"One other thing."

"What is that?"

"You're going to the village."

"At the point of a gun?" Deneen half smiled. "I think not. And we'll stay as long as I choose to."

"If you do, you'll stay alone."

"Madora is under my command. If I stay, he'll stay . . . and with all of his men!"

Turning to go, Flynn said quietly, "Ask him."

Twenty

•

They waited in the darkness crouched low in the mesquite, watching the pines off across the clearing. Clouds had formed in the night sky and now the moonwash was a soft haze that barely outlined the dense shape of the trees.

Madora said, "How long now?"

"About twenty minutes," Flynn answered.

"That's not so good."

"Maybe they're close and he can't move."

Deneen, crouched at Flynn's right, moved his leg and his boot scraped the loose sandy rock.

Madora's head turned. "Why don't you ring a bell?"

Deneen began, "Madora, you'll be sorry you ever . . ."

"Damn it—shut up!"

Indicating the pines across the clearing, Flynn said, "That's where the Mimbre was killed . . . maybe he's run into something."

"Like the other two," Madora said.

Flynn glanced at Madora. "If he doesn't show soon, we'd better start thinking. What about the rest of your trackers?"

"They'll wait a good hour before following: give us plenty of time. If something happens, they're on their own."

But a moment later, Three-cents appeared, crawling, squirming into the mesquite. He told them that two Mimbreños were among the trees looking for the one who had disappeared, feeling through the pines carefully. "They will look only a short time more, searching a wider area. Then they will go to inform the others."

"Which means," Flynn said, "we go now or never."

"What did he say?" Deneen whispered, demanding, not merely asking.

"He said it's empty; we could drive a wagon through," Madora told him.

"That's not what he said!"

Madora did not bother to reply; he moved out and they crawled single file after him across the clearing, moving more quickly through shoulder-high brush hands and knees again across another open stretch and then into the pines. They waited, listening to the silence, then deeper among the trees they could hear crickets. They sing if nothing's disturbing them, Flynn thought. But even a cricket wouldn't hear a Mimbre. They moved on, creeping through the trees, brushing pine needle branches, holding them from swishing . . . and three of them gritted their teeth and felt needles down their spines as Deneen's boot snapped a rotted tree limb. They stopped where they were and dead silence followed.

Three-cents looked at Madora and when the scout nodded he moved off, disappearing into the darkness.

The clasp knife is in the left side pocket, Flynn thought, and his hand moved against the cloth feeling the shape of it. He could feel the weight of the pistol beneath his left arm. But no shooting, he reminded himself. He smelled the cold fresh smell of the pines and suddenly he realized there was no longer the sound of crickets. A movement in the tree darkness flicked in his vision.

He saw it again, a short quick shadow movement, and held his gaze on it, waiting for it to show again. When it did, he knew that it was a man, and almost instinctively he knew it was not Three-cents.

He glanced at Deneen. He hadn't seen him. The shadow moved again, coming closer cautiously, taking the definite shape of a man. It went through Flynn's mind: Joe's closest. It's up to him. Now he could see the shoulder-length hair and the colorless gray of the breechclout. He knew Madora, a few feet in front of him, was ready; but now he thought of Deneen, behind, slightly to the side, and he wanted to warn him not to move, but he knew it was too late. Joe—get the mouth. Whatever you do, don't let him yell. Let him take a few more steps—

"Oh God!" and the pistol shot slamming the stillness on top of the words.

Deneen held the pistol out in front of him . . . the Apache was on the ground . . . but suddenly another shape was coming out of the trees . . . his thumb hooked the hammer and he fired at it . . . the figure hung motionless and he pulled the trigger twice again until the shape dropped to the ground.

Madora's voice suddenly—hoarse, urgent, "Stop him!"

Flynn was moving . . . one hand gripped the gun barrel, wrenching it from clawed fingers . . . the other tightened in uniform cloth to drag Deneen to the ground.

"Get off of me!"

The face beneath him was tight with panic, ready to scream again. Flynn pushed his palm down viciously over the mouth, holding it there, seeing the eyes stretched open—

Madora was next to him. "He shot Three-cents!"

"What!"

"The second one . . . it was Three-cents! The crazy son of a bitch killed him!"

Looking down, seeing the eyes, Flynn's hand tightened over the jaw. And one of the flashes in his mind, coming through the shock of Madora's words, said: This would be easy. But it was momentary. Ten years on the frontier was telling him something else, something undeniable, urgent

. . . and he leaped up to follow Madora who was already moving, running through the trees. They reached the end of the trees together and paused, drawing their pistols. Then they were in the open—five, six, seven strides—and suddenly the gunfire broke, coming from three sides, pin-point bursts of flame, stopping them in their tracks, forcing them back crawling, lunging into the cover of the trees.

Minutes later, after the firing had stopped, Deneen appeared. He said it once. "Goddamn it they all look alike. How did I know who it was?" That, by way of an apology.

Flynn could still feel the hot anger and he thought: Now that he's said that, he can forget about it. He's explained and apologized in one. Life is very simple. Why do you let it get so complicated—just look at it the way Deneen does. And within the first few minutes he also thought: Take your anger and use it now against these Mimbreños. But he felt the closeness of the trees. No, it would be all right if you were fighting them in the open, with fists; but there's no place for anger here. They'll come at dawn and if you're still excited, two minutes later you'll be dead.

They moved a few yards to where there was more protection—the brush was heavier and a fallen tree formed a natural barrier on the side that faced deeper into the trees, and out from it there was a fifteen foot clearing to help some. The other side looked out on the open meadow they had started to cross. Flynn remembered that the next trees were about two hundred yards off, with Soyopa's cemetery beyond them. The threat was not from the open side.

Madora moved next to Flynn.

"They'll come soon as there's a hint of light."

Flynn nodded.

"How would you figure it?" Madora said.

"Come from the inside, through the trees. If they can count to five three times they've got us."

"Be all over before we could reload."

"Did you take Three-cents' gun?" When Madora nodded he said, "That'll help some. How many rounds you got?"

"About thirty, plus the loads in Three-cents' gun."

Flynn patted his coat pocket. "That's about what I got. Will they count shots?"

"Hell yes. What side do you want?"

Flynn was closest to the fallen tree. He said, "Well, now that I'm here." He glanced at Deneen who looked away quickly.

"Then you get this," Madora said, handing him the extra pistol.

"If you want to use it sometime, it's all right."

"Maybe next week," Madora said.

Now Flynn was looking out past the fallen tree, his eyes probing the darkness and the trees. There! Did you hear it? There must be a lot of them if they make a noise. The Coyoteros will be pinned down; there aren't enough of them to do anything. Twice he thought he saw movements, but he held his fire. Wait for the real thing, that will come soon enough. The time was passing and he knew it would not be very long and he was as certain as he could be that he would die within the next hour. You have to have time to reload. O my God I'm heartily sorry for having offended Thee. I detest all my sins because I dread the loss of heaven and the pains of hell; but most of all because they offend Thee, my God, Who art all good and deserving of all my love. I firmly resolve with the help of Thy grace—

There!

His left pistol came up and fired. Count them! One. Another shape coming across the clearing, stumbling with the report. Two. A Mimbre darted from one tree to another and he missed him. Three. Don't throw them away! The same one came on, in view for a longer time, and he knocked him flat. Four. Madora's firing the other way. Don't look around. There . . . off left! The slamming report and powder smell. Five. Now wait . . . you're starting to reload . . . here they come!

He stood up suddenly, pointing the other pistol, firing, seeing them go down . . . four blasts from the pistol and two Mimbres dropped, one hit twice. Others were coming out of the trees! No . . . split-second indecision and they were going back in. Hurry up, reload! He inserted two cartridges, looked up, and when there was no movement he loaded three more; then the other gun.

The firing had stopped on both sides. "What did you have, Joe?"

"Ponies. Didn't you hear them?"

Flynn shook his head.

"They were for attention," Madora said. "Your side's the one."

"Don't tell me."

"You want to trade off?"

"I'm used to it now."

Turning toward Deneen, Madora said, "You want to help out next time?" He stopped, his eyes narrowing into a frown. "You feel all right?"

Flynn looked over. Deneen was crouched with his back against the base of a pine, half hidden by the branches, clutching the pistol in a tight-knuckled, close-to-chest, protecting way as if it were the only thing that stood between him and the end of his world. And the picture of that night at Chancellorsville flashed through Flynn's mind—the darkness and the dripping pines and almost the same tight-jawed wide-eyed expression frozen on his face—and Flynn looked away, back to Madora.

"We're not going to get any help from him," the scout said. He looked out over the meadow in the dawn light. Flynn moved back to the fallen tree, but as he did Madora called, "David, look-at over there."

His eyes followed Madora's outstretched arm through the early morning haze, out across the meadow. There, at the edge of the trees two hundred yards off, stood three Mimbreños. They were looking toward the pines; then one of them motioned and others appeared, carrying something.

"David . . . that's a man."

Flynn studied them, watching two warriors drag the limp

form of a man between them. They held him upright then while another Mimbre threw a line over a tree limb above them. Flynn saw now that one end was fastened to the man's wrists and as the Mimbreños walked off holding the free end, the line tightened, drawing the man's arms up over his head and the next moment he was hanging above the ground.

Madora said, "Do you recognize him?"

Flynn shook his head. "His head's down."

"Get Deneen's glasses."

Deneen was staring at Flynn as he turned toward him. "What is it!"

"Take it easy. Let me have your glasses."

Deneen's left hand felt the case hanging at his side. "I'll look first!"

Flynn shrugged. "You won't like it." And he thought: He's not as bad as at Chancellorsville. Maybe he thinks there's still a way out.

Deneen looked through the glasses. When he brought them down his face was drawn tighter than before and for a moment Flynn thought he was going to be sick. Madora jerked the field glasses from his hands without ceremony. "He told you," the scout said, and handed the glasses to Flynn; and after he had given Flynn time to study the man he asked, "Who is he?"

Flynn lowered the glasses, handing them back to Madora. "I don't know. His head's still down . . . what's left of it."

Looking through the glasses Madora said, "Scalped. And nekked as a jay-bird." He was silent. Then, "He's alive, David."

"You're sure?"

"Positive."

"What's that?" Flynn watched the Mimbres nearing the man again.

"They got knives," Madora said. He grunted. "You see that?"

"Enough," Flynn said quietly.

"They cut the tendons in his arms." Madora waited, and winced holding the glasses to his eyes. "Now both his legs."

Deneen turned away.

Flynn said, "That's for our benefit."

"You bet it is." Madora lowered the glasses. "They're telling us what's coming up about an hour from now."

"Next time they'll rush until they get us," Flynn said.

Madora nodded up and down. "The first time they found out what they wanted to know . . . though it cost them more than they figured. Your side was the natural, cuz of the cover, just fooled around mine. Next time they'll come mounted, all of them . . . like a twister and run right through us."

Flynn didn't know what to say, but he said, "Well . . ." and in his mind, rapidly: . . . but most of all for having offended Thee, my God, who art all good and deserving of . . . "Joe, what if we run?"

"Which way?"

"Back." He nodded into the trees.

"We wouldn't get ten feet." Mildly, Madora said, "David, the only thing we can do now is think about all the things we shouldn't of done before."

Flynn half smiled now, thinking of Nita. "And all the things you'd like to have done."

"What would you do, David, besides kick his francis from here to Prescott?" He nodded toward Deneen.

Flynn said vaguely, "Maybe stay around here."

"And prospect?"

"Maybe."

"For what?"

Flynn smiled. "She's a nice girl."

"I thought so," Madora said. "Well . . . it'd be a nice living." He looked at Deneen again. "And I wouldn't see how you'd have anything further to prove as far as he's concerned."

Flynn said, "Only nothing like that will happen now." Still,

he thought of Nita Esteban, until she was forced suddenly
from his mind—

"David . . . here they come!"

Flynn had time to recognize Soldado, though it was a
quick, fleeting glimpse—first Soldado, then his warriors riding out of the trees, coming out bunched, separating in the
open, the rumble of their ponies, dust rising—then he was
whirling back to face the dense pines. He heard a pistol shot
close behind him, but it went in and out of his mind for he
was tensed waiting for something else, then Madora's
voice—

"David!"

Nothing moved in the trees. He glanced around quickly
seeing Madora and beyond him the Mimbreños swerving
their ponies, racing down through the wide aisle between the
pines and the trees they had come out of.

"They don't want *us!*"

And off to the left, far out, were mounted men. They had
been coming along the road that, ahead, would skirt the
cemetery, but now momentarily they stood holding their
horses, almost a dozen riders, watching the Apaches bearing
down on them . . . then as one they spurred, breaking for
the village off beyond the trees.

"They were waiting for them all the time!"

"Joe, that's Lazair's men!"

"God Almighty they don't have a chance!"

"Joe!"

Madora's head jerked toward Flynn, seeing him pointing
off to the right, the other direction, and as he followed
Flynn's gaze his eyes opened in amazement.

"God Almighty . . . *rurales!*"

Flynn screamed through the din of the horses that had
swerved around from the right side of the trees, "And Bowers! Look at him!"

And there it was. Cavalry! Cavalry out of the Manual.
Charging, full-glory cavalry used the way it should be, the
way you dream about it but seldom see it. Something out of

Cooke's Tactics. And it was all there as Flynn had seen it before—only here were straw Chihuahua hats and the full-throated battle screams were in Spanish. Flynn felt the excitement in him and screamed at them as they rode by bearing down on the Apaches who were milling, turning in confusion and not all the way around when Bowers hit them. He hit them with gunfire, carbine butts, sabers and a will . . . a rawhide cavalry will to hit the enemy, slash him hard in the first few seconds and use the rest that makes up a minute to mop up, chase the stragglers, run them to the ground.

And as suddenly as it had started, it was over. Some Apaches, perhaps a dozen, had broken free and were streaking off in the distance; many were on the ground, horses and men, scattered over the meadow; and there were those who had given up. They sat their ponies sullenly with their hands raised in the air, herded into groups, rurales circling each group with carbines ready.

Then Bowers was coming toward them, holding his mount to an easy trot, the saber flashing in the sunlight; but he saw the naked figure hanging from the tree and he guided the left rein in that direction.

Madora was grinning broadly in his gray-streaked beard. "Where'd he get that saber? David, I think he might do."

Flynn was smiling, but then he turned quickly remembering Deneen . . . there, by the tree. "Colonel . . ." The word hung by itself with none to follow. Flynn stared, feeling the cold shock of what he saw, then gradually realizing what had happened—remembering the pistol shot right after Madora had yelled that the Mimbreños were coming.

That was enough, just knowing they were coming, and knowing what they would do from seeing the man strung up across the meadow. That finished him, Flynn thought. At Chancellorsville it was a shelling. That had been bad. But what the Mimbreños had in mind would have been much worse. So . . .

"Joe . . . look here."

Madora was silent for some time looking at Deneen

slumped against the tree. The face was beyond recognition, the pistol barrel still jammed into his mouth, his hand still on the trigger. Then Madora shook his head slowly. "When did he do that?"

"Right after you yelled. I remember hearing a shot close, but I thought it was you."

Madora shook his head again. "Just think, if he'd a put that off one minute he'd be bitchin' at us for something right now."

"Maybe," Flynn said, "he's done everybody a favor."

Madora said, looking up, "Here comes Bowers," and moved out to the edge of the trees.

Flynn started to follow, but he stopped, glancing back at Deneen thinking of Bowers. What good would it do him to see that? Flynn thought. Throwing it in his face that Deneen was a coward . . . *a Colonel, United States Cavalry.* And suddenly he had hurdled the fallen tree trunk and was dragging back the nearest of the dead Mimbreños, lifting him over the trunk, dropping him to the other side, dragging him up face-down over Deneen's body. He pried Deneen's hand open, closed the Mimbre's fist around the gun butt and placed the barrel back—gently—against the gaping teeth-shattered expressionless hole.

Madora was calling, "Red, where in hell did you get that sword?"

Bowers was dismounting as Flynn reached him. He pushed the sword point into the ground, taking the extended hand, grinning, feeling the glory of it, but not wanting to show his excitement.

Flynn smiled back at him, saying, "There was no room for cavalry, but it was cavalry that won after all. How'd you do it with Santana?"

Bowers smiled half self-consciously, even in his cavalry pose, hand resting on the sword hilt. "Santana and I talked for a long time last night," he said. "We discussed again the battle of Cinco de Mayo at Puebla. We talked of Santana's military ability—about which he wasn't the least bit restrained—then we got around to Gettysburg—the second day, if the memory of my father's words serves me correctly —and I told him about an incident during the Culp's Hill skirmish."

Bowers squinted. "Now I think it was Geary's division of Slocum's XII Corps holding the hill, with Ewell's rebel division pinning them down. Ewell couldn't climb his division up the hill, but neither could Geary get out . . . and Meade, that's General George G. Meade, wanted part of Geary's division over to reinforce Sickles' end of Cemetery Ridge where Longstreet was hammering. Now there was a fellow named Gregg with some cavalry sent to help out Geary, but he couldn't see how to get at Ewell, until, from the hill, they spotted a supply train coming up along Rock Creek. They knew Ewell's scouts would tell him about it and from then on it was timing. Ewell started for the supply wagons and Gregg hit him while his pants were down with umpteen troops of Union Cavalry." Bowers' eyes were alive, smiling. "I've always considered that would have been some sight to see." He said then, "Now just casually I mentioned to Santana, 'If Lazair's men were to come down that road in the morning, Soldado would sniff him and it would be pretty much the same maneuver, wouldn't it? And for a military man of your ability, it would be easy as walking.' That did it. He even dug sabers out of Duro's storeroom. We knew the Mimbres were in the trees . . . no other place they could be; so we waited until there was a sign of Lazair's men far out, then swung out a side street and barreled around that grove of trees."

"How did Duro react?" Flynn said.

"Duro's dead. He ran for it during the night. Hilario was watching then . . . he told him to stop, but Duro kept going, so he shot him. Hilario said someone else ran out ahead of Duro. We've been trying to figure out who it could be." Bowers jerked his thumb over his shoulder vaguely pointing across the meadow. "We didn't even think of him, but that's who it must have been."

From Flynn, "Who is it?"

"Lazair."

Flynn paused, surprised. "Is he dead?"

Bowers nodded. "Dead as a stone."

Madora half smiled in his beard, noticing the new, sure-of-himself tone of Bowers' voice along with the hip-cocked cavalry way he stood. He said, "Red, you might do at that . . . with a little seasoning."

Bowers smiled, though he was thinking: Damn, how you have to listen to old men and smile just because they are old men. As if a few more years just naturally makes them wiser. Then he said, because he had to say something, "I hope so, Mr. Madora. I do hope so." And then, remembering, Bowers said, "Where's the colonel?"

Flynn stepped aside and nodded into the trees and followed Bowers as he walked in among the pines.

"My God—"

Flynn said nothing. And suddenly, watching Bowers' face, he was more than glad he had done this—seeing the young lieutenant looking at a soldier's death—no, more than that, looking at a *colonel of cavalry* killed in action. When a colonel dies, it's a bigger thing, Flynn thought. No matter how he dies.

Bowers was saying, "This will head the report," his voice heavy with respect, "for it isn't often that a colonel dies this way."

Flynn looked at him quickly, but only awe and respect were on Bowers' face and Flynn said, "No, thankfully, it isn't often."

Madora came up behind them. He glanced at Flynn after looking down at Deneen, but he said nothing to him. Then to Bowers, "I see Soldado survived . . . him and about two dozen others. Counting his women up in the hills somewhere, you'll have about seventy people all told. Red, how do you propose to get 'em to San Carlos?"

"I was thinking of talking Santana into helping as far as the border . . . have cavalry come down to meet us there."

Bowers smiled. "Hell, Joe, all the fight's out of those Mimbres. The three of us could take them up, for that matter."

"You mean the two of us."

"Two?"

"David here's talking about doing some prospecting."

Flynn smiled, but he didn't deny it.